🦋 100 🦋 DRESSES

If the Magic Fits

100 DRESSES
If the Magic Fits

Susan Maupin Schmid

Illustrations by Lissy Marlin

Random House 🏠 New York

Text copyright © 2016 by Susan Maupin Schmid
Jacket art copyright © 2016 by Melissa Manwill
Interior illustrations copyright © 2016 by Lissy Marlin

All rights reserved. Published in the United States by Random House Children's Books, a division of Penguin Random House LLC, New York.

Random House and the colophon are registered trademarks of Penguin Random House LLC.

Visit us on the Web! randomhousekids.com

Educators and librarians, for a variety of teaching tools,
visit us at RHTeachersLibrarians.com

Library of Congress Cataloging-in-Publication Data
Schmid, Susan Maupin.
If the magic fits / Susan Maupin Schmid ; [illustrator, Lissy Marlin]. —
First edition.
p. cm. — (One hundred dresses ; book 1)
Summary: Darling Dimple, a young orphan, discovers a closet full of magical dresses, each of which gives her the appearance of another person in the castle and that, along with her own magical abilities, helps her protect Princess Mariposa from betrayal as the castle swarms with suitors.
ISBN 978-0-553-53366-8 (trade) — ISBN 978-0-553-53367-5 (lib. bdg.) —
ISBN 978-0-553-53368-2 (ebook)
[1. Fairy tales. 2. Courts and courtiers—Fiction. 3. Magic—Fiction.
4. Clothing and dress—Fiction. 5. Orphans—Fiction. 6. Identity—Fiction.
7. Humorous stories.] I. Marlin, Lissy, illustrator. II. Title.
PZ8.S2835If 2016 [Fic]—dc23 2014044370

Printed in the United States of America
10 9 8 7 6 5 4 3 2 1
First Edition

Random House Children's Books supports the
First Amendment and celebrates the right to read.

For my daughter Sara,
a connoisseur of all things fairy tale

1

I wasn't born in a tower or in a golden chamber. I wasn't born a princess or even a lady. But I *was* born in a castle built by dragons. Not that you would think so to look at it. Perched on the side of a mountain, the castle blazed like a diamond in the sun—majestic, but ordinary as castles go. You wouldn't suspect that it had anything to do with dragons. Or magic. But it did.

My mother was an Under-chopper, working beside the Under-slicer in the castle kitchens, when she had me. My father was a sailor who'd been lost at sea. My grief-stricken mother spent her days chopping vegetables and sobbing. The day I was born, she kissed me good-bye, curled up her toes, and died. The Under-slicer, Jane, plucked me from my departed mother's side. She squinted nearsightedly at my wrinkled red face.

"What a Darling Dimple!" she exclaimed.

I'm told I screamed at this pronouncement, but it did me no good. The name stuck. Everyone from the Head Steward down to the Stable Boys called me Darling Dimple. Never mind that I didn't have a dimple. Nor was I particularly darling. My hair flew around like the white fluff of a dandelion. My skin was pasty, my nose stubby. My eyes were the color of water, which is to say they had no color whatsoever. Some folks said they were gray, some blue, some green. Roger, the Second Stable Boy, said they were yellow. But *he* didn't know anything.

For all her nearsightedness, Jane taught me to read, write, count, and wield a whetstone. She had a soft spot for me the size of a plum pie. When I was small, I followed her around the kitchens. I'd hold a corner of her apron in one fist and a wooden spoon in the other. Just in case one of the cooks had a sudden need for a taster. As I grew older, I helped her: fetching vegetables from the bins, keeping count (if the Soup Chef said twelve onions, he meant twelve), and sanding the chopping block. At the end of the day, when every knife was sharpened, Jane took me upstairs to sit at the paws of one of the great bronze lions guarding the lower gardens. We gazed at the stars with the other Under-servants, dreaming of far away until it was time for bed. We slept in a room tucked under the kitchens where the air carried a hint of cinnamon and spice. But all that changed.

When I was ten and Jane's eyesight had dwindled to the near end of her nose, she accidentally cut off the tip of her finger. The Head Cook retired Jane from his service. The Head Steward gave her a new position with the Pickers, who gathered flowers from the gardens and arranged them in great bouquets for the Princess's tables. Jane was happy in the flower-scented sunshine. But I was too old to follow Jane around the gardens.

The Head Steward called me to his office. I stood quaking before his broad, polished desk. He sat ramrod-straight, drumming his desk with a pencil, his crimson uniform dripping with cords and tassels.

"Well, well," he rumbled, "what shall we do with you?" Dark eyes studied me from under bushy eyebrows.

I gulped. I couldn't very well say that I wanted to do something big, something important. Something *grand*. A grand job would be exciting, an adventure. Ten-year-olds weren't offered *grand* jobs.

"Yes? Speak up." His pencil beat the polished wood.

I caught my reflection in the surface. Some poor Under-duster spent hours slaving away with a rag and lemon oil to produce that sheen. I rubbed my elbow in sympathetic pain. I did *not* want to be an Under-duster—or an

Upper-duster, for that matter. Dust was dust wherever it might be.

The Head Steward rustled through a stack of papers, then pulled one out, clearing his throat.

"I could do Jane's job," I blurted out. I imagined myself surrounded by the savory smells of roasting meat, simmering spices, and baking bread, happily slicing carrots for the casserole. It wasn't exactly grand, but it wasn't dusting either.

"Under-slicer, sir," I added, in case he needed reminding.

He blew his great bushy mustache out with a snort. "Under-slicer! Under-slicer, indeed." He wagged his pencil at my nose. "You're too young for such a lofty position as Under-slicer."

"I—I was a b-big help to J-Jane," I protested, my vision of bubbling stews evaporating.

"You—girl—have to work your way up from the bottom just like everybody else."

I repressed a groan—by bottom he meant the under-cellar. It was dark in the under-cellar. The Head Steward scribbled a note on a piece of paper. "Take this to the Head Scrubber," he ordered.

I bobbed a hasty curtsy and trudged off, holding my note like a soiled rag. The Head Scrubber, or the Supreme Scrubstress, as those in the under-cellar called her, was famous for her lack of imagination, and *she* was my new boss. Scrubbing was the lowest job in the castle—and the least exciting.

The Supreme Scrubstress gave me a cot in a corner with a hook for my apron and a small wooden crate stamped ARTICHOKES, where I could keep my treasures. Had I any. Which I didn't. So began my life in the under-cellar. The cellar was packed with barrels, stacked with crates, lined with racks of wine bottles, and stuffed with sacks of potatoes. There was enough to feed everyone who lived in the castle, both the court upstairs and the servants below. Under all that, down a rickety wooden stair, was the under-cellar, a place of oil lamps, cobwebs, fires burning in great hearths, and vats of steaming water for scrubbing. Pots and pans went to one side and laundry went to the other.

I worked on the pots side in a steamy, soap-bubbly nook. Lye, soot, and ash stung my nose, like notes in a strong perfume. Warmth from the steaming water colored my cheeks a rosy hue and curled my wispy hair. My fingers wrinkled like prunes. Even though I wore my apron and rolled up my sleeves, I was wet most of the time. Droplets condensed out of the steam onto my hair. Splashes from my vigorous scrubbing dotted my skirt. It had to be vigorous—the scrubbing—because the Supreme Scrubstress was apt to patter up behind one on tiptoe, brandish her monstrous wooden-handled sponge, and swat an unsuspecting Scrubber on the behind to emphasize the sort of vigor she required. Her swats packed a wallop.

"Dar-LING!" she called in her shrill voice. Hair from her unraveling bun writhed around her face like tiny snakes. Her second chin wagged with her outrage; the rolls around her middle jiggled with her displeasure. "Stop daydreaming and put some muscle into it!"

I'd bob my head and say, "Yes, ma'am. I'll scrub harder, ma'am." There was no point in arguing with her. Simply put, nothing less than well-applied elbow grease would dent the baked-on residue in the pots and pans. The sooner I worked my way through my share of pots, the sooner I could escape to the cool of the night air and indulge in a daydream or two.

I was lucky that I got to scrub pots—the cooks sent the pots down as soon as the food was ladled into the serving bowls and platters. I was skip-happy free once I'd hung up my apron. The poor dishwashers had to stay up until everyone had eaten and then wash their way through towering stacks of dishes, bowls, cups, and platters.

The first blaze of green spread over the gardens and, *wham,* a wave of feasts followed. Feast days were the worst; they lasted for hours. Every suitor for miles around came to the kingdom of Eliora by the White Sea to woo Princess Mariposa. Well, why not? Princess Mariposa had hair as dark as midnight, eyes as changeable as the sea, skin as white as snow, and lips as red as cherries. Or that's what the poets wrote. She was very pretty. And she had the whole kingdom all to herself. That's the sort of princess that even the laziest suitor will pursue. But every new suitor meant a boatload of work for the servants, from boot-polishing to dusting to laundry to . . . you guessed it, pots!

The trail of pots down the rickety wood stairs was never ending. My fingers wrinkled to the bone, the steam peeled the tip of my nose, and my elbows creaked with the effort. Soap bubbles rose in the steamy air, shimmering in the lamplight. I'd lift my sponge and touch one, lightly, just enough to set it rolling in the steam, careful not to break it. Then I would picture myself in the soap bubble, Darling the Mighty Sailor.

I held fast to the rigging of my schooner, a spyglass in my free hand. A distant island beckoned her misty green fingers across the roaring sea. A fair jewel ahead! I'd set a course for her and pry her treasures loose from those fingers. Ahoy! But the sea had other plans. Towering waves rolled the ship, pitching her from side to side. On the deck, my crew cried out to me to turn back.

"Sail on!" I crowed back at them. The wind tore at my hair. The sea spit foam. A clutch of black rocks leered at me from between the waves, gnashing their sharp teeth, anxious to tear into the tender planking of my schooner's side. I signaled to the wheelman. To starboard! To starboard! Gritting his teeth, he hung on the wheel, spinning her with all his might. The timbers creaked. The masts moaned. The sails whistled.

The prow of my schooner slicked past the rocks—by an inch.

The sea screamed in rage, but calm waters rode ahead. And the island held her breath, awaiting my arrival.

It was a very pretty daydream indeed. All shimmery and glistening while the bubble lasted. And while it wasn't a real adventure, for a moment in the sooty dimness of the cellar, it made me feel that my life was as grand as Princess Mariposa's.

Well, almost. While I scrubbed pots by lamplight, the Princess spent hours scouting the countryside for rare butterflies. Her collection filled an entire room, but still she prowled the woods, clutching a net, scrambling through bushes and over briars, a trail of servants behind her. All the while, the possibility of another rare butterfly fluttered just beyond her reach. The servants might grumble as they picked burs out of their stockings, but they'd say that if the Princess wanted a *Polyommatus bellargus,* well then, she should have one.

Princess Mariposa wore a crown that twinkled with diamonds, ate off golden plates, drank from crystal goblets, and rode in a golden carriage. She had a castle full of servants, a kingdom full of subjects, and an army of soldiers—all to please and serve and protect her. She had everything a princess could need or desire and *more*.

Because deep under her castle-built-by-dragons, in the under-cellar, she had a secret weapon: me, Darling Dimple.

But she didn't know it. And up until then, neither did I. She was about to need a secret weapon and I was about to have the kind of adventure I'd dreamed of. Long afterward, she herself told me how on a feast day while I was scrubbing pots in the under-cellar she was wrinkling her pretty nose at the state of her petticoats. And that's how my adventure started, with Princess Mariposa's pretty wrinkled nose.

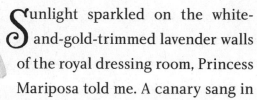

2

Sunlight sparkled on the white-and-gold-trimmed lavender walls of the royal dressing room, Princess Mariposa told me. A canary sang in a gilded cage. The thick green carpet caressed the soles of the Princess's feet as she wiggled her toes. Usually the Princess awoke beaming like a ray of sunshine, but this morning a slight cloud hovered about her. She fidgeted impatiently as Cherice, her Wardrobe Mistress, tied the innumerable ribbons that accompanied the Princess's underclothes.

In an effort to coax a smile from her, Cherice said, "Did you hear, my dear? Several new suitors arrived late last night. One, I'm told, is a prince—Prince Baltazar—and very charming."

"Mmm," Princess Mariposa said, absently toying with a ribbon and untying it.

Cherice eased the ribbon out of her mistress's fingers and tied it again. "Indeed. Very charming. *Especially* charming. I'm told he has chiseled features and very broad shoulders."

"He sounds like a statue," the Princess replied.

The truth is that Princess Mariposa had been keeping the kingdom all to herself for some little while. Years had passed, scores of suitors wooed her, but none had pleased her. There were grumblings in the court that she could not be pleased . . . and that she would never marry. And, worst of all, there would be no prince or princess after her to inherit this wonderful kingdom. It didn't much concern us in the under-cellar, but the rest of the kingdom was growing more worried with each passing month.

Cherice bit her lip, mulling over a suitable compliment to pay this latest prince, one that would pique Princess Mariposa's interest. "I'm told he's terribly clever."

"Then we should set this statue prince at the gate—he can impress everyone who enters the castle with his wit."

Cherice frowned. "My dear, one must look for something good in others or one will never see it."

"There must be something there to see. Chiseled features. Charm. Cleverness. All very nice qualities in a prince, but I'm looking for so much more than that." Princess Mariposa sighed; her lips trembled and her eyes grew misty.

"Sometimes one must make do with whom one can find, my dear," Cherice said.

"A prince," the Princess murmured, "who is brave and true. One who can see into his beloved's heart and discern its most secret wish."

Cherice rolled her eyes. "I wish that there *was* such a prince," she said.

Princess Mariposa whipped around to face Cherice, untying another ribbon in the process. "Should any princess settle for less?"

Cherice had the duty of dressing the Princess and having her ready on time every morning, every afternoon, and every evening (in those days princesses wore a lot of clothes), and any delay threatened to put her behind schedule. She smiled and caught the errant ribbon.

"My dear Mariposa! If ever a princess deserved such a prince, it is you," Cherice assured her. With that, she tied the last ribbon, bobbed a quick curtsy, and dashed to the wardrobe hall. She returned with a new lavender silk gown over her arm.

It was at that very moment that Princess Mariposa wrinkled her pretty nose.

Princess Mariposa stood before a mirror dressed in

her very best silk underclothes, trimmed with lace and bedecked with ribbons. And plagued by wrinkles—not the adorable wrinkling the Princess's nose did whenever she was annoyed. No, these were the disorderly sort of wrinkles that infest poorly ironed petticoats.

"This," Princess Mariposa said, "will never do. My new summer gown will never lie smoothly over this—this—" She pointed to the looking glass. "LINDY!" the Princess bellowed, causing the crystals in the chandelier above to tinkle. (The Princess possessed a very strong set of lungs.)

Lindy, the Head Presser, appeared at the doorway leading to the pressing room, where all the Princess's clothes were ironed. She propped a fist on her straight hip and flipped her straight hair out of her eyes. Everything about Lindy was straight and smooth. Rumor had it that she pressed herself with one of the Princess's irons every morning before breakfast.

"What would you *call* this, Lindy?"

"Well, Your Highness, I'd call that a betrayal, that's what. A flat-out dereliction of duty. The twisted work of a wicked sloth—"

Cherice smoothed the ruffled flounces on the petticoat. "My dear, I'm sure there has been some unfortunate incident. The iron, perhaps, was too cool. Or the petticoats were scrunched in the hanging. Some silly little thing. I am sure."

Lindy pinked up with indignation and a smidgeon of guilt. Normally she saw to the final pressing, being zealous about the Princess's wardrobe. But the evening before, she had left the task to her assistant while she flitted off to—but I'm getting ahead of myself. Let's just say that Lindy hadn't done the final pressing, she'd trusted—

"Faustine!" Lindy exploded. "Trust an Under-presser just once and see what happens!"

Princess Mariposa blinked. This was an ominous sign. Blinking usually led to frowning, which often led to the Princess stamping her foot. When that happened, you knew she was really, truly angry. Cherice and Lindy held their breath. Princess Mariposa blinked again. The wrinkle in her nose reached her forehead.

Princess Mariposa rubbed her wrinkled forehead. "Perhaps I should lie down. I feel the tiniest little headache behind my left temple."

Cherice eyed the little gold-painted clock on the wall beside her. It was nearly time for the feast to commence. "Now, my dear, think of all those long faces at the banquet when you don't appear! The *new* suitors will be so disappointed."

"Forget them," Princess Mariposa snapped.

Cherice flinched.

"Well then, that dashing Earl of Westerfield," Lindy offered.

"He. Waddles."

"Count Ruthven?" Cherice suggested.

"Stumpy." Princess Mariposa rubbed her forehead more energetically.

"Prince Armand?" Lindy said.

"Conceited."

"Prince Steffen?" Cherice's voice had an anxious note in it.

Princess Mariposa put her face in her hands and spoke through her fingers. "He has the face of a toad, the manners of a pig, and the mind of a flea."

This was the rudest thing Princess Mariposa had ever said. Cherice and Lindy exchanged shocked looks as the little gold-painted clock ticked quietly away.

"I am sorry that Your Highness has had to make do with such uninspiring suitors. But if you won't go down and meet these latest . . ." Cherice trailed off meaningfully. "I suppose you could always bow to your late father's wishes and marry Prince—"

The Princess dropped her hands, eyes flashing. "Don't say that name!"

"—Humphrey." The name popped out before Cherice could stop.

Humphrey hung in the air of the dressing room like a damp petticoat on a laundry line. The Princess closed her eyes, balled her fists, and counted to ten. Prince

Humphrey's father and Princess Mariposa's father had gotten the two of them together one summer when they were nine. The two kings hoped that they would enjoy each other's company, eventually fall in love, and marry when they grew up. The kings had been sadly disappointed; no two people disliked each other more thoroughly. Prince Humphrey and Princess Mariposa hadn't spoken since.

Lindy grimaced at Cherice, who shrugged. Said was said and couldn't be unsaid. But Lindy, not being one to endure a long silence, spoke up. "Oh my goodness, Your Highness, I'm sure it won't come to that. There must be one okay fellow—"

Princess Mariposa nailed Lindy with a look that would parch the bubbling-est brook. For a moment, no one spoke; Cherice held her breath. Then the Princess, gathering her dignity and banishing all thoughts of Humphrey, said, "Take this petticoat and see that it is properly pressed at once!"

"I'll see to it personally," Lindy said, bobbing a curtsy.

The Princess signaled to the Wardrobe Mistress to untie the petticoats. "*See* that you do. And, Lindy."

"Y-yes, Your Highness," Lindy said.

"I never want to hear the name Faustine again."

"Yes, Your Highness," Lindy and Cherice echoed. They exchanged a look. They needed to find a new Under-presser—and fast.

3

eanwhile, in the under-cellar, a fat soap bubble glistened on the tip of my sponge. A cloud of steam fogged the air. Gillian, the Under-dryer, leaned on her elbows over the vat, a thick towel around her waist, and put her chin in her hands. The rising steam tightened her dark curls and cast a dewy sheen over her cheeks. Her naughty grin dimpled her heart-shaped face.

The Supreme Scrubstress had paired us up because we were the same age. And close in height—I was taller—which made handing things off to be dried quicker. Quickness was highly prized by Her Supreme Scrubself. Gillian and I had worked together for a year, washing and drying our way through a mountain of pots, and a bubble on the end of my sponge was a signal of an irresistible sort.

"What do you see?" Gillian asked.

Glancing around to be sure we weren't overheard, I said, "I see a lone tower on a hill and a knight standing below it."

"Yes?" Gillian's eyes sparkled. She was a sucker for a good story.

"In the tower lives a great enchantress so powerful that—"

"Is she beautiful?" Gillian prompted.

"Very. No one can resist her charms. And so powerful that . . ." I trailed off, stopping to examine the bubble.

"Yes, yes, go on," Gillian breathed, gripping the vat's edge.

"The elixir she brews can mend anything." My voice died to a whisper. "Even broken hearts."

Gillian's mouth made a perfect O. She straightened up and clasped her hands over her heart.

"The knight has a broken heart!" she cooed.

I smiled, for I saw myself in the tower holding the vial of elixir aloft. If Sir Knight wanted his heart mended, then he must come to me, Darling the Great Enchantress.

Gillian nudged me. I took a deep breath for emphasis.

"The knight is a famous dragon-slayer," I said.

"Ooh, a dragon-slayer," she echoed. "What happens next?"

"The knight enters the tower and throws down his sword. 'I will give all I have for this potion,' he cries. The great enchantress smooths her very golden hair and holds the vial out to the knight. 'Sir Knight, in exchange for my elixir I must have the scale of a golden dragon,' she says."

"Scale of a golden dragon," Gillian said. "Imagine."

"The knight vows he will slay the next golden dragon he sees, and so she gives him the elixir—"

"Argh," a voice gargled. "The potion burns!"

A sandy-haired head popped up on the side of the vat, accompanied by a battalion of sandy freckles. Roger the Second Stable Boy, Freckled Wonder of the World, gripped his throat with both hands and made choking noises, staggering back and forth.

"Aw, stop," Gillian said, "you're ruining it."

Roger grinned and lolled against my vat as if it were his. "Good thing I did; Darling was about to waste your time with another of her silly daydreams."

"It wasn't a daydream! It was a story," Gillian said.

"I've got a story for you," he said with a laugh, "about a valiant Second Stable Boy and his trusty shovel—"

"Be off with you," Gillian said, leaning dangerously over the vat to cuff Roger's ear.

Roger ducked as she swung, leaving Gillian teetering on the vat's rim, flailing her free arm, trying to maintain her balance. I grabbed her collar and hauled her back with one hand while keeping a careful grip on my bubble-topped sponge with the other. Roger rocked with laughter. I steadied Gillian, eyeing His Freckleness with a baleful glare. Nearly falling into a vat of scalding water was no laughing matter.

"Do you smell something?" I asked Gillian.

She sniffed the air and shook her head. Puzzled. Not taking the hint.

I held my free hand over my nose. "I think it's horse manure. Look at his boots!"

Her eyes lit up and she gagged, pinching her nose shut. "Thmell arful!"

"Go away," I told Roger, wagging my sponge at him as the soap bubble bobbled precariously. "And take your stinky horse smells with you!"

"We work hard out in the stables. You Scrubbers splash around all day, blowing bubbles," he said with a scowl, and poked my bubble with his freckled finger. The bubble burst, sprinkling my stubby nose with its dying gasp.

"Roger!" I shrieked, and brought my sponge down on the top of his head.

Which was just what he deserved, but the sponge was full. The impact of it on Roger's head sent a blast of hot water straight into Gillian's face. She screamed and covered her eyes with her hands.

"Are you okay?" I asked her.

She answered by jumping around and shrieking like a teakettle with a hot bottom. In the distance, I heard the pounding of feet on the stone floor. More trouble was on its way. Roger glared at me, wiping the water off his face. He had a cap in his hand that he dipped into the scalding water and prepared to fling at me.

So I did the sensible thing. I ducked. And the cap full of steaming hot water sailed over my head. Behind me, I heard a splat and someone exclaim, "Oof!"

I peeked over the vat's rim. Roger grew pale. Gillian dropped her hands. Her face was red where the water had hit, though her eyes were untouched. She gulped and turned a worrisome shade of sea green. I wasn't so sure I wanted to see whomever she and Roger saw, but I turned slowly around.

The Supreme Scrubstress stood there panting, red-faced, and dripping. This would have been bad enough if the water had been fresh, but I had scrubbed quite a few pots in it by this time. A nasty brown stain spread across her starched white apron. A tremor started in the Supreme Scrubstress's second chin and rippled through each roll around her middle, down to her shoes, which began tapping a staccato rhythm. She quivered with fury.

I swallowed hard.

Up came her monstrous wooden-handled sponge. She pointed it straight at Roger. "You," she said. "Get. Out. Of. My. Cellar."

Roger choked, torn. For underneath the fierce tapping

of the Supreme Scrubstress's shoe lay his soggy green cap. It was the same cap all the Stable Boys wore—and were required to replace should they lose it. I happened to know that Roger didn't have any money to spare.

"Now!" the Supreme Scrubstress roared, and took a swing at him with her sponge.

Abandoning his cap, he dived out of her way. Straight into a stack of freshly washed and dried pots. The pots rattled and clanged as they tumbled onto Roger and over the wet floor. One hit Gillian on the knee. "Ow!" she cried, clutching her knee and hobbling in circles. "Ow! Ow! Ow!"

"You," the Supreme Scrubstress said, pointing at me. "I'll teach you to moon about when there's work to be done." She raised her sponge again. I braced myself.

"Ahem." A delicate cough came from behind us. "We were looking for the Head Scrubber."

A lady dressed in the bluest sky-blue gown stood there, twirling a magnifying glass she wore on the end of a long silver chain. Her hair was piled high on her head, which accentuated her long neck. She was fair and pretty. The lady next to her was tall and as stiff as an ironing board.

The two dwarfed the Supreme Scrubstress, who drew herself up as tall as she could, banished her sponge behind her back, and smiled. I had never seen her smile before. And I would be thankful if I never saw it again. For her smile was not only big and wolfish, it was full of gold-capped teeth.

"I am the Head Scrubber. Marci, at your service," she purred.

Marci? The Supreme Scrubstress had a name? No one I knew had ever called her by it, and I knew pretty much everyone under-cellar.

Roger, who wasn't nearly as stupid as he looked, took this opportunity to snatch up his cap and crawl away toward the stairs. I let him go. I knew where to find him.

"Excellent, my dear. I am Cherice, the Wardrobe Mistress, and this is Lindy, the Head Presser. We require a helpful—"

"De-pend-able!" Lindy put in.

"Dependable girl to assist in pressing the Princess's things," Cherice said.

Gillian immediately ceased her clatter, all bright-eyed and perky, ready to volunteer. But before she could speak, a fire lit in the Supreme Scrubstress's eyes. Marci, Her Supreme Scrubself, smiled at me—the sort of smile that certainly couldn't mean anything good—and turned to Cherice. I swallowed hard for the second time that morning.

"Pressing, eh? Hard work that requires close attention, eh?" the Supreme Scrubstress asked. I did not like her tone.

"There's no shilly-shallying in my pressing room," Lindy said.

"And will this new—ah—Presser be well supervised?" the Supreme Scrubstress asked.

"Watched like a hawk."

I cringed.

"No idling. No mooning about." The smile on the Supreme Scrubstress's face grew till it threatened to invade her second chin. "No daydreaming?"

"I should say not!" Lindy said.

"Indeed not," Cherice added.

"Then I have just the girl!" the Supreme Scrubstress said. She reached back, seized me by the arm, and fetched me over to the Wardrobe Mistress. "Darling is the girl for you!"

I gasped, dizzy with fear and excitement. Gillian sniffled in her disappointment. Clearly, she felt the wrong girl had been chosen. For a moment, I thought so too. This new job sounded like . . . well, all work and no fun. More so even than pot-scrubbing. And pot-scrubbing left a lot to be desired in the fun department.

"Excellent," Cherice said, clapping her hands.

"She'll do," Lindy said. "Darling?" she added, as if she thought she hadn't heard right.

"Darling Dimple." The Supreme Scrubstress's multiple chins bobbed in assent.

"A nice name," Cherice said.

Lindy frowned slightly but didn't argue.

"Curtsy to your new mistress, Darling," the Supreme Scrubstress said.

I did. And that was how I got out of the under-cellar.

2

The upper-attic floated in a world high above the under-cellar. I'd been over every inch of the cellars, kitchens, lower gardens, and the castle's main floor. I'd flitted into the ballroom, the galleries, the great hall, and even peeked into the throne room to gape at the marble swans holding up Princess Mariposa's throne. But I'd never been higher than the first floor. The trip to the upper-attic lasted staircase after staircase after staircase, up and up, until my knees began to wobble and my breath came in puffs.

Not only was the upper-attic high in a tower, it gleamed with light. Everywhere I turned, a window greeted me and sunshine caressed me. The white walls glowed. The polished floors shone. Even the doorknobs flashed me brassy winks. Despite the fact that we climbed the servants' stairs and not the wide marble stairs the Princess used, we passed white-and-gold colonnades, arches, rooms painted in jewel tones, and corridors painted in mouthwatering pastels. I had no idea the upper servants worked in such beautiful places. I couldn't wait to tell Gillian. She'd be so jealous her curls would tighten right into corkscrews.

I tilted my head back, steadying an imaginary crown, as I ran a hand along a polished banister. The Princess would spot me pressing her clothes and see in me the friend she'd always dreamed of. We'd spend all our time together. We'd tell each other our secrets. She'd simply *order* me to wear a little silver crown so that everyone would know how special a friend I was.

"Right in here," Lindy said, smacking a door and knocking me out of my daydream. "The girls' dormitory, your new home."

She opened the door on a bright yellow room lined with plump, eiderdown-covered beds. A rag rug lay by each bed. A jar of violets sat on a windowsill. There were no cobwebs anywhere.

I stashed my wooden crate stamped ARTICHOKES under the bed Lindy pointed to. She'd told me to fetch my things. I was too ashamed to admit that I hadn't any, so I'd brought my crate. I figured that as long as I kept the lid on it, no one would know it was empty. I slid it deep under the bed, crawling halfway in to do so. There were no dust bunnies under there, no mice droppings, nothing. The floorboards felt as smooth and clean as the inside of one of the kitchen's best copper pots.

"That's the new Under-presser," I heard Lindy say.

"Ah. And she's wearing what?" a voice answered.

I slid out from under the bed, dusting my apron off even though it didn't need it.

"That's the under-cellar uniform. She'll need clothes and boots," Lindy answered.

A slight girl stood next to Lindy. She eyed me and my brown dress and tan apron with disdain. She wore a silver-gray dress and a crisp white pinafore with a gray butterfly embroidered on the pocket. Her dark braids swished as she shook her head.

"I had no idea they dressed like that," she said as if I had on a potato sack and some dirty laundry. "I'm Francesca," she said, pointing to her chest and speaking slowly. "I'm the Head Girl. All the Princess's Girls take their instructions from me."

"Well, this one's mine," Lindy said shortly. "I need her ready within the hour." With a nod to me, she turned on her heel and marched out.

Francesca put her finger to her chin. "One hour. My, my. I can't work a miracle in one hour, now can I?" She sighed. "What's your name?"

I licked my lower lip. Under-cellar people knew my

name and the story behind it and no one minded much. But a glance at Francesca's wide gray eyes and arched brows stilled my tongue. I was tempted to call myself Sally or Cora or Lucy, anything but Darling.

"Your name?" Francesca prompted.

"Dar-dar—" I stuttered.

"Darla?"

Temptation seized my wrist, twisting. It would have been so easy. All I had to do was nod, and my name would become Darla. Not that I was fond of *Darla,* but it had the virtue of being a nice, normal, boring name. Everyone in the upper-attic would call me Darla and no one would ever know . . . I paused, mouth open. The Supreme Scrubstress had told Lindy my name was Darling; she'd certainly call me that. Sooner or later Francesca would find it out.

I gulped.

"Well?" Francesca rolled her eyes. "Darcy? Darlene? What is it?"

"Darling," I said in a small voice, dropping the Dimple like a dead rat. *Sorry, Jane.*

"Darling?" Francesca's eyes widened. Her cheek twitched. I could tell I was never going to hear the end of it.

I stood, stretching as tall as my legs would stretch. "Darling," I said with a sharp nod. As if it were normal to be named Darling.

"All righty, Darling," she said, smothering a smile.

"Let's find you clothes." She waltzed over to a tall cupboard and flung open the doors. In a moment she turned around with a folded pile of gray and white cotton. "Here you go. Change and leave your . . ." Her lip curled. "Leave those *old* clothes on the floor. I'll have someone send them back downstairs."

I held the fresh clothes and waited for her to leave. Minutes ticked by. Francesca folded her arms. Clearly, she was not about to give me any privacy. So I turned around, pulled off my apron and dress, and stepped into the new dress. The fabric slipped on like butter over toast and smelled like lilacs. The pinafore had wide sashes that tied behind my back. I fumbled with them for a moment until Francesca whisked them out of my hands and whipped them into a bow.

"You'll get the hang of it," she told me over my shoulder, and went back to the cupboard. After a little digging, she produced a pair of gray boots. "Try these."

I sat on the edge of the bed and yanked off my old boots. My big toe poked through the front of my brown stocking. I shoved my foot into my new boot, not looking up to see the expression I was sure was on Francesca's face. But she had already moved away and was rummaging through a dresser.

"Ah," she said, producing a fat gray ribbon. "Tie your hair down with this."

I shook my head. "It won't stay."

She smiled ever so slightly. "Tie it anyway."

I took the ribbon and slicked back my dandelion-fluff hair. As soon as I attempted to knot the ribbon around it, it began slithering away. A wisp dangled before one of my eyes. I snatched at it.

"No," Francesca said, taking the ribbon from me. "Like so." She pulled my hair back and slid the ribbon around the top of my head and tied it underneath my hair. When she released the hair, it danced around, but stayed out of my face. "There, now you won't scare the Princess."

"Scare—" I gulped.

"Well, you're not like the *other* girls who serve Her Majesty," Francesca said.

I felt a hard nugget lodge in my throat. My daydream shriveled. The other girls looked like Francesca—pretty, polished, and self-assured. The Princess would take one look at me and my dandelion hair, stubby nose, pasty skin and—

"Don't worry." Francesca patted my shoulder. "Lindy keeps her helpers busy. The Princess will probably never even *see* you." She gave me a little shove. "Run along. Lindy's waiting."

I took a step and stopped. I had no idea where to go. I wrung my hands, feeling dumb and silly in my new silver-gray dress.

Francesca sighed as if the weight of the upper-attic rested on her shoulders. "Go down the corridor. Take the first stair on the left and then the second door on the right."

I walked across the room, repeating to myself *first stair left, second door right.* I pulled the door open by its shiny brass knob and stepped into the corridor. Over my shoulder, I heard Francesca call, "Good luck, *Darrrling,*" followed by kissing sounds and a muffled giggle.

My ears burned like red-hot rinse water. I tore off down the corridor, away from that muffled giggling, as fast as I could go. I saw the first stair on the left and raced down it. I whipped around a corner, pulled open the second door on the right, and leaped through. Smack-dab into a corridor lined with identical white doors. I took a couple of steps . . . first stair left, second door on the right . . .

Had I gone down the right stairs? Picked the right door? In my haste, I had no idea if I had. This certainly wasn't the pressing room. I'd have to backtrack and try again. I turned around and realized with a jolt that whatever door I'd come in through had swung closed. Door after door marched down the walls on either side of me like suspicious sentinels. I had no idea which door was the right one.

I'd just have to open them all.

5

A long time later, I sat curled up on a step. My hair had pulled loose from its ribbon and tendrils drifted down my forehead. I was lost. Not confused or a little turned around; lost. Francesca's directions had taken me nowhere. I had found myself in a deserted tower. A tower where no one ever came. A tower that probably had a witch hiding at the top. I had no idea how to get where I was going and no particular urge to climb up to find the witch.

I imagined myself sitting there until I turned into a sad little skeleton. Some maid would eventually sweep me into her dustbin. Poor Jane would never know what became of me. I sniffled, picturing Jane's anguished, nearsighted searching of dark halls and dungeons. She'd call,

"Darling, oh, Darling, where are you?" as she lifted a candle to pierce the murky cobweb-shrouded halls—

"There you are!" Cherice said, tapping her palm with her magnifying glass.

"I—I'm l-l-lo—" I sputtered.

"Lost," Cherice finished for me. "Yes, I see." She pulled a hankie out of her pocket and handed it to me. "Let me guess. Francesca gave you directions."

I nodded and blew my nose. "She said to take the first stair on the left and then the second door on the right."

"Yes. Well. Let that teach you. Never, *never* listen to Francesca. Come along. Lindy will be"—she paused—"annoyed. Yes, Lindy will be very annoyed."

She made *annoyed* sound a whole lot more like murderously furious than just a little irritated. I shuffled after her. She rounded a corner and plunged down a stair.

"We have a map on the pressing room wall. Use that to get where you're going," she said.

"I—I'll explain to Lindy that Francesca said—"

"No." Cherice shook her head. "Don't tell anyone. Trust me, my dear. If Francesca finds out you were lost, it will only encourage her." She walked through an arch and up another stair.

Cherice walked across a landing and opened one of a set of big double doors, all white and trimmed in gold and painted with the royal crest. Inside was a wide room with soft gray carpet and tall, twisty candlestands. A large mahogany desk, bulging with papers and thick white leather-covered books, guarded the entrance. On each side of the room were doors with gold numbers on them. One, two, three, and four were to the right. Five, six, and seven were to the left. At the end, I spied a gray room lined with ironing boards. The pressing room.

"Lindy, my dear, here is your new Presser," Cherice called, and pulled a set of keys out of her pocket.

I twisted my fingers together behind my back and waited to see how *annoyed* Lindy would be. Not a sound came from the pressing room. A bead of sweat ran down between my shoulder blades. My shoulders ached from standing stock-still. Cherice clanked her keys impatiently.

"Well, she must have stepped out for a moment," Cherice said, and unlocked door number two.

I gasped. Inside door number two was a long narrow room with a stained-glass window at the end that threw pink and green shadows on the white walls. Rack after rack of shoes lined the room. I drifted after Cherice as she went inside. The racks were arranged by color, like a rainbow. I turned around and around. Teal. Apricot. Violet. Black. Crimson. Jewels. Buckles. High heels. Low heels. Silk, satin, leather, patent, gold brocade . . . the shoes dazzled me with their beauty. And their numbers! So many shoes for one princess!

"Ah," Cherice murmured, selecting a pair of dove-gray velvet slippers with pink satin bows. "There you are. I've looked everywhere for you." She grimaced. "Nobody, and I mean nobody, puts anything away in these closets but me. Nobody."

"Nobody," I echoed.

Cherice smiled and gestured at the shoes. "Amazing?"

I nodded, fingers twitching to *touch* a shoe or two. Or five.

"Come along," she said, and hurried out of the closet. "Number one," she said with a gesture, "underthings. Number two: shoes. Number three: gloves, parasols, and scarves. Number four contains everyday dresses. Number five: formal dresses. And number six: ball gowns."

"Wow." Princess Mariposa had *six* closets. I wrinkled my forehead. "What's in number seven?"

"Oh," Cherice said, waving seven away. "We don't even bother to lock number seven. It's full of *old* dresses."

I blinked. "Old?"

"See here," she said, throwing open the door. "These belonged to the Princess's grandmother, Queen Candace. All dated, all terribly out of style."

"Oh." I pressed my palms to my cheeks. Before me was a long closet with a thick floral carpet and a peaked-arch window. In the window's center shimmered a canary composed of thousands of slivers of bright yellow glass. The canary was so lifelike that any moment you expected it to flutter its tail feathers and sing.

"Yes. Well, look around, my dear. Lindy will be back any minute," Cherice said, and walked back to her desk.

"Okay." I stepped into the closet. On either side, dress after dress hung on silver hangers. Each hanger was crowned with a gold badge that featured a number. I touched the soft folds of the royal-blue silk dress hanging from Number Thirty-Six. Darker blue velvet wrapped the bodice with its pinched waist; diamonds sparkled on the shoulder. *This* was old-fashioned? I shook my head; if I had a dress like this, I'd wear it.

But then, Princess Mariposa had three closets filled with dresses. I shrugged and riffled my fingers through the brilliant fabrics. There had never been such beautiful dresses. I spied lace and ribbons, ruffles and embroidery, velvets, satins, and wonderfully figured brocades. Forty-Eight glowed, a deep forest-green velvet, embroidered with holly and crimson berries and sporting a laced bodice and pointed sleeves. Fifty shimmered in a cascade of silver lace. I turned at the canary and crossed to the front of the other side. Seventy-Seven was a lilac satin with silver ribbons and a silvery white underskirt. Eighty-Two was a twist of scarlet and orange scarves sewn together to resemble flames.

Flame-colored slippers peeked out from beneath the skirt's folds. The ninetieth hanger held a sunshine-yellow dress with a garden of ribbon flowers scattered across the skirt.

Dress One Hundred was white, speckled with crystals and embroidered with doves and roses. Lace fell from its sleeves and pooled on the floor underneath. A wedding gown, I was sure. I imagined Queen Candace wearing this to marry King Richard, bouquet in hand, smile on her face. I buried my face in the soft satin, inhaling the whisper of fragrance still clinging to the fabric. Orange blossoms, roses, and vanilla . . .

"Dora—Delcy—Delilah! What's-your-name, wake up!"

I whirled around. Lindy stood in the closet's doorway, a hand propped on her hip, a cloak over her arm. Her face glowed and her eyes sparkled, as if she'd been out in the sun and wind.

"Darling," I said. "My name is Darling." I braced myself to see just how *annoyed* she was.

"Well, Darlin', it's time to get to work," she said, and turned on her heel with a flounce.

For a moment, I held my breath, but I heard her whistling. Not the sharp whistle you'd use to call a dog, but the whistling of someone having a very good day. I exhaled; if she was *annoyed*, it didn't show. With a longing glance at the hundred dresses, I trotted after her, too relieved to wonder where she'd been.

6

Someone opened the curtains, splashing sunlight all over my face. I squeezed my eyes closed and tugged the covers higher.

"Rise and shine!" Francesca called.

I heard the slithering and scrambling of girls getting up to greet the morning. A hand snagged my covers and flicked them off me.

"Wake up, Darrrling!"

I heard a chorus of snickers. Holding back a sigh, I opened my eyes. They were all waiting for me, holding their aprons or their hairbrushes, bright-eyed and eager. I sat up and put a bare foot on the floor beside my bed. Gritty sand rasped under my toes.

"What's this?" Francesca asked in mock surprise.

"More sand? Where does it all come from?" She clicked her tongue. "Clean it up before you go."

A red-haired girl handed me a broom as the roomful of girls giggled. "Wash behind your ears," one called. "Empty your boots outside," said another. "Don't worry, you'll get the under-cellar out of your skin one of these days," added a third.

It was their morning routine. For the past five nights, I'd fallen into a bed laced with sand. Every night, I'd been too tired to do anything more than sweep it off the sheets and onto the floor, only to be handed a broom the next morning. So far, I'd swept up the sand without saying anything. Not accusing anyone of planting the sand. Not screaming or yelling or throwing the broom at them. I remembered what Cherice had said about encouraging Francesca. I was pretty sure throwing a fit would please her more than anything.

"I do hope this stops soon or I will have to speak to the Head Steward about it," Francesca said, tying a ribbon on the end of a braid.

"Ooooh," the girls moaned in mock sympathy.

A chill ran down my spine. Francesca might make me miserable, but the Head Steward could take away my job and send me packing. I had no parents, no home other than the palace, and nowhere to go. My lower lip trembled.

A tear formed in the corner of my eye. Jane would die of heartbreak, worrying about poor little me lost out in the big cold world.

"Be sure to sweep under the bed, just in case it"—Francesca paused to shudder—"travels."

"Oh, sweep under my bed!"

"Mine too."

"Mine!"

My fingers curled around the broom handle. I would not cry. I would not be fired and break Jane's heart. My spine snapped into a straight line. My mouth hardened. I swept up the sand as the rest of them got dressed and ate breakfast. The sand had indeed traveled to every corner of the room. Francesca must have gotten up early and scattered more. By the time I was done sweeping, the girls had gone. I jumped into my clothes and snatched the last roll off the breakfast tray. I crammed it into my mouth as I raced down the halls. I skidded into the pressing room just before Lindy could notice I was late. Again.

Luckily, Lindy was nowhere to be seen. The empty pressing room echoed with the sound of my footsteps. A basket piled high with old towels and sheets stood waiting for me. I took a deep breath and smoothed my apron, touching the pocket and making sure my paper was still there. Cherice had given it to me to copy the map on the pressing room wall. With my own little map in my pocket,

I hadn't gotten lost a second time. At least there was one nice person in the upper-attic.

Lindy was determined that I practice my way to perfection before she'd let me take an iron to anything that might touch Princess Mariposa's snow-white skin. I'd been practicing for five days, ironing the same stack of tattered and stained discards. I fed coals into the little stove under the three heavy wooden-handled irons she'd assigned me. They had to be hot, but not too hot. And you had to work fast because they began cooling off the minute you took them off the stove. That was why there were three of them; you could always switch your cooling iron for a hot one.

I tossed a towel with a large silver-gray monogrammed *M* onto my ironing board, picked up the shaker bottle, and sprinkled water on the towel. I rolled it into a log and set it aside, reaching for another. Cloth had to be moist when you put the hot iron on it or it would scorch. I sprinkled and rolled only the number of pieces at a time that I could iron before they dried. Lindy had taught me that rolling them helped them stay moist longer.

When I was ready, I unrolled a damp towel and picked up an iron. The fabric sizzled and a cloud of steam billowed up as the metal touched the cloth. *Tell the Head Steward.* Huh. I could tell the Head Steward a few things, like the girl who slept in the bed next to me had candy hidden in her pillowcase. And Lindy disappeared with her cloak two or three times a day. She never said that she was leaving or where she was going or when she'd be back. Just, *poof*, she was gone, leaving me alone to iron this same stinking basket of old stuff over and over.

A part of me missed the under-cellar. Not the pot-scrubbing but the familiar rooms and faces. I missed Gillian and Jane and all the kitchen servants I'd known my whole life. I missed fitting in.

Maybe tomorrow a new ship would sail into the Princess's harbor. Blazing white sails. Deck laden with treasure. A tall man waving from the bow. "Ahoy," he'd call. "I'm looking for my daughter."

"You must mean Darling Dimple!" the people gathered on the wharf would cry.

And they'd lead him straight up the mountain to the palace.

The smell of toasting cloth touched my nostrils. I bit off a gasp and yanked the iron away. A triangle of brown smoldered on the old towel, right through the silver-gray *M*. I glanced around with a guilty gulp, but still no Lindy. I wadded the ruined towel up in my hand. Lindy hated wrinkles. Hated them. But she hated scorch marks even more. Scorch marks made her straight hair curl as she boiled with rage. I'd seen Lindy angry once, when I burned a hole in an old pillowcase, and I did not want to see it again. Too

many scorch marks and I'd never get to press anything for Princess Mariposa. I'd be sent to the Head Steward. . . . I gulped again. I doubted the Supreme Scrubstress would be in a hurry to take me back. I could picture the tall palace gates opening and a soldier shoving me outside into a blizzard. Would they let me keep my silver-gray dress and new boots? Or would I have to hobble off, barefoot and shivering in my underthings?

The iron winked at me in the sunlight. Oh, yes. It was summer outside. I'd have to hobble off barefoot and sweaty. I scrunched up my face; not nearly as romantic a scene, that. Oh, well. No poor little orphan like me should lose her job over one ratty old towel.

I looked around for a place to hide it. The stack of unused laundry baskets? A Laundress might see it. And raise a ruckus. Behind the big stove where Lindy heated her irons? It might catch fire. The cupboard where she kept her cloak? First place she'd find it. No, I needed to hide it somewhere Lindy never went. I inched closer to the door to the wardrobe hall with its seven closets. I could hide the towel somewhere in there. Cherice might see it, but she was too kind to tell on me.

To get there, I had to make it past the doorway into the dressing room, where I could hear Cherice helping Princess Mariposa dress. Up till now, I'd only caught glimpses of the Princess gliding past doors, wearing gorgeous

clothes. Pale violet. Turquoise. Rose-petal pink. The rings on her fingers flashed as she went. I had strict orders from Lindy to stay put in the pressing room, so Princess Mariposa had never seen *me*. Just like Francesca predicted. My daydream about our becoming best friends had yet to materialize.

The door was open a crack, so I decided to take a peek. I took in the green carpet and the white and gold trimming the lavender walls, the birdcage stand in the corner. The canary chirped in the cage next to the lavender curtains.

Princess Mariposa stood turning back and forth before a mirror, a cloud of raspberry silk drifting with her. Crystals dripping off the skirt cast prisms on the walls. Cherice stood nearby with a pair of raspberry-colored gloves in her hand. I squinted and wedged myself more tightly to the crack, ears wide open.

"Does this seem a little . . . intense for morning?" Princess Mariposa asked.

"It's perfect for a luncheon, my dear. You look tempting enough to bake in a pie," Cherice said.

"Wonderful. I will be mistaken for dessert and poked with a fork," Princess Mariposa said tartly, and ruffled the crystals at her neckline. "Will there be anyone new today?"

Cherice dangled the gloves in the Princess's direction.

"I had not thought to tell you this, my dear, not wanting to alarm you—"

I held my breath, anxious for what might alarm this beautiful raspberry-gowned lady.

"Go on," Princess Mariposa said. "Alarm me." She reached for the gloves and began to slide one on her satiny white hand.

A tinkling laugh came from Cherice. "My dear, you are a wit. A young man dressed in worn clothes did come to the gates last night. He claims to be a prince, impoverished, obviously, but still—a prince."

I exhaled with a sigh. A prince, that was all. Not an evil wizard or a fire-breathing dragon or an ogre with a club the size of—

"An impoverished prince?" Princess Mariposa's eyes sparkled. "How romantic."

"Naturally, he was not invited to today's luncheon," Cherice added. "Not with so many fine suitors in attendance."

No indeed, I thought, some *penniless* prince had no business bothering my beautiful Princess. Seriously, how would he drape her in diamonds and lavish her with . . . whatever luxury princesses ought to be lavished with? I wrinkled my forehead trying to imagine what luxury Princess Mariposa could be missing out on.

"Send for him!" Princess Mariposa exclaimed.

At that, the canary began to sing with gusto. Deep down, I knew that now was the moment for me to be on my way, but I was glued to that crack.

"Hush," Princess Mariposa admonished the canary, and turned to Cherice. "Instruct the Steward to seat this new prince next to me."

"M-my dear," Cherice sputtered, "that very handsome and clever Prince Baltazar was promised that *he* would sit next to you today."

"Well, I suppose I have *two* sides, don't I?" Princess Mariposa snapped. "Put that poor prince on my right and Prince Baltazar on my left."

The canary went wild, flapping frantically at the thin gold bars of his cage, singing out louder than before.

"What has gotten into him?" Princess Mariposa said, clapping her hands—one covered in a raspberry glove and one bare—over her ears.

"I don't know," Cherice replied as the canary grew still louder and more frantic. "I've never seen it behave this way."

"Take him away!" Princess Mariposa called over the bird's cries.

Cherice hurried over to the stand, lifted the cage off its hook, turned around—and saw me peeking in the door. She marched toward me. I backed away, thrusting the towel behind my back. She barged through the door and shoved the cage at me.

"Do something with this *now* or I'll tell Lindy that you've been spying!"

I dropped the towel and took the cage. Cherice slammed the door shut in my face. The canary stopped his outburst so quickly that my ears were still ringing as I stood there with the birdcage handle twisting in my sweaty grip. The canary cocked his yellow head and regarded me with bright black eyes as if to say, *What's that towel doing on the floor?*

Lindy came in at that moment, swirling out of her cloak, and dancing it into the cupboard. While her head was safely tucked into the cupboard, I scooped up the towel and stuffed it between me and the cage. The canary blinked at it curiously, dipping his head and opening his beak. I shushed him with a finger before my lips.

"What have you there?" Lindy asked, emerging from the cupboard and tying on her apron.

"Um," I said.

"Is that Princess Mariposa's bird?" Lindy asked, the threat of a frown hovering on her lips.

"Yes. Cherice told me she wants her canary taken away," I said.

"No, she doesn't. She's had a canary in her dressing

room since—forever, it's always been there. Her mother had it."

"The same one?" I said, wondering how long canaries lived.

Lindy propped a hand on her hip. "Now, how should I know? I have a pack of work to do and so do you." She wrinkled her nose. "Do you smell something burning?"

"Nope." I inched a step closer to the door to the wardrobe hall.

She walked over and rooted through my drying towels. "Huh. Well, find a spot close by for that bird. Knowing the Princess, as soon as you get rid of it she'll want it back."

I slipped another step closer to my escape. "I—I—I'll just put it in a closet for now."

"Hmm . . . ," Lindy said, sniffing at the air around my ironing board.

I darted into the wardrobe hall. I jiggled the handle on door number one. Locked. Probably all the closets were locked. Cherice had the keys. I couldn't very well go into the Princess's dressing room and interrupt to ask for the keys. I thought a minute. Door seven, Cherice had said, was never locked. I twisted the knob on number seven and the door opened. The canary chirruped in the cage.

"Do you like this one?" I asked.

He chirruped again.

"I do too," I said. I spied a table tucked in the corner

near the window and walked over to it. The table teetered on spindly legs. The inlaid top looked like it would scratch easily. "Just a minute," I told the canary, and set the cage down on the carpet. I whisked the scorched towel over the tabletop, picked the cage up, and set it down.

"Two birds with one stone," I said. Then I blushed at the canary's quizzical stare. "Not like that. I would never kill a bird. No, I just meant that the towel will protect the table, and *you* with your pretty cage will protect me from anyone finding my towel."

The canary flicked his tail as he took this in. He seemed to decide that everything was all right because he trilled a couple of notes and cocked his head at the window. I looked straight into the beautiful glass canary. I wondered if Queen Candace had had a canary of her own as well. I leaned against the window ledge. My fingers bumped against a crank.

"Would you like some air? It's a little warm in here."

Cheep-cheep.

Turning the crank opened a side panel and let in the fresh summer breeze. I peered out. The head of a stone gryphon appeared beneath me, one of the gryphons that perched on the battlements overlooking the Princess's gardens below. I patted the gryphon and turned back to the birdcage. The canary smoothed his ruffled feathers, stretched his neck, and sang. Silvery notes filled the room.

And then something truly magical happened. The dresses stirred as if they'd been asleep and were just now waking up. As the canary sang, ghostly arms lifted the dresses' sleeves, and their skirts swirled. The hair on the back of my neck prickled; goose bumps rose on my arms. The dresses danced on their silver hangers as if beckoning me to join them. My toes twitched. My heart skipped along with the notes of the canary's song. I rubbed my eyes. Dresses do not dance. They hang quietly until someone wears them.

I looked again. The dresses shivered expectantly, a jewel glittering here, a lace flounce waving there. The canary cocked his little yellow head and blinked at me with eyes like black diamonds. What on earth did he want? Expectation weighed in the air around me. The terrible sensation that I ought to *do* something pinned me to the floor. Do what? The canary had air and food and water, and the dresses had . . . hangers. What else was there?

"Darling!" Lindy's call pierced the silent wanting of the closet and snapped me out of the moment.

"I'll be back," I promised the canary, and bolted out the door.

7

That night I fell into bed like a stone and slept until a *thump* jarred me awake. I lay still and listened intently, wondering what had woken me. The only sound I heard was the breath of sleeping girls whispering in the darkness. I rolled over on my side. Then a *swoosh*ing tickled my ears so softly that I wondered if it was real or just the sound of my own pulse. I listened harder, but all was quiet. All manner of critters lurked in the under-cellar, but no rat or beetle or spider would dare show its face in the upper-attic— I had to have imagined I'd heard something. Yawning, I burrowed back into sleep.

I woke again to a little *bump* under my bed as dawn glowed behind the white curtains over my head. The breaking light pushed through the thin cloth and lit the floor below. The clean floor. The polished, bare, sand-free floor. I sat straight up, rubbing my eyes with my fists. I looked again at the floorboards beside my bed. They had been swept as clean as—as if the Supreme Scrubstress had been at them with an army of Scrubbers. Last night, I'd shaken the sand out of my sheets and onto that floor just like every other night.

Someone had swept the floor.

But who?

I slid out of bed and tiptoed to the waste bucket to check for the sand. And found it empty. *Empty.* If someone had swept up the sand, where was it now? I stood scratching my head as Francesca bounced up and rallied the room. Girls poured out of their beds and began getting ready for the day. Francesca waltzed over to exclaim about the mess beside my bed and—stopped short.

I strolled to the cupboard and pulled out my clothes. As if nothing had happened. Francesca blinked. Her mouth popped open and closed like a fish. One of the girls giggled. She glared at that girl, and the giggle turned into a cough.

"Hurry up, girls," Francesca said in a voice that did not welcome discussion.

I took my time, taking forever to pull on my socks and lace my boots. I lingered until every other girl had filed out of the room. I had to know if that *bump* I'd heard was real. So breakfast roll in hand, I knelt and peered under the bed skirt. The only thing under the bed was the box stamped ARTICHOKES. I reached in, snagged the box, and slid it out. Holding my breath, I inched the lid aside.

Pale sand drifted across the bottom of the box like a miniature desert. Tucked in a corner, cozy and quiet, was a little family of plump white mice. Five in all. The largest twitched his whiskers and *winked* at me.

"Did you sweep the floor?" I asked, realizing how dumb it was to be talking to a mouse: a little furry creature who couldn't possibly talk back. But the mouse nodded solemnly.

I rocked back on my heels. I pinched myself hard on the arm just to be sure I was awake.

The mouse rolled onto his hind legs. Then with one paw over his furry chest, he bowed.

I rubbed my eyes with my fists, half expecting the mouse to be gone when I looked again. But he was still there, waiting, front paws clasped, tail at the ready.

"Why?" I asked. The mouse flicked his long pink tail at the sleeping mice beside him. "For your family?" Again, the mouse nodded.

Feeling a little dizzy and a little crazy, I broke a piece off my roll for the mouse. *My* mouse. I laid the bread in the box. "Thank you," I whispered, and slid the lid back in place and pushed the box back under the bed.

I walked through the upper-attic, running my fingers along the walls, reassuring myself that the castle was solid. Real. I pinched myself again. I was solid and real and awake. Had I really met a sand-sweeping mouse? I thought I had. I stopped and stuck my head out of a window for a breath of fresh air. All the green and gold of the mountainside lay below. The vivid blue sky hung above. The wind whispered. One of the stone gryphons waited impassively. It was real. And solid, I thought as I patted its head.

And there hadn't been any sand on the floor, much to Francesca's dismay. I grinned. That was real for sure.

When I reached the pressing room, Lindy was gone. So I went to feed and water the canary. Holding my breath, I opened the closet door. The hundred dresses trembled on their hangers as if they were anxious to see me. What could they want from me, the Under-presser? Tickling with a hot iron? They didn't look to me as if they needed any pressing. They looked as bright and fine as the day they'd been hung up. Whenever *that* was.

The canary cheeped merrily as I slid out his little dishes to fill them. Behind me, the dresses held their collective breath. *Nonsense.* They didn't have any breath to hold. Cloth. Thread. Buttons. Laces. Nothing more. I marched past the dresses with my chin up, pretending I didn't even know they were there—and went back to work.

I sighed at the sight of my workstation—another day with the never-emptying basket of old rags—and fed the stove under my irons. Cherice popped in and tossed a handkerchief on my ironing board.

"Quick, press this and bring it in," she said, and raced back to the dressing room.

I stared at the crumpled bit of silk. I smoothed it out, tracing the pattern of embroidered butterflies along the edge, fingering the elegant *M* in the corner. Lindy would hang me out with the stone gryphons if I scorched this.

Bring it in, Cherice had said. Press this and bring it in. I swallowed—here was my chance to take a handkerchief I'd pressed straight to the Princess. I licked my forefinger and gingerly tested one of my irons. The metal sizzled as the moisture touched it. I snatched my hand back. I picked up the water bottle and sprinkled the handkerchief. With gritted teeth, I glided the iron over the surface of the fabric. The wrinkles melted like snow. I folded the square and pressed it into a rectangle. I folded it again and pressed it into a little lilac square with an *M* in the corner. Perfect.

I set the iron down. I cradled the warm handkerchief in my palm like a baby chick and walked to the dressing room door. Inside, Princess Mariposa stood before the mirror, turning this way and that in orange silk. Lindy knelt at her feet, struggling with tiers of ruffles. The

Princess's gown was ruffled at every turn—from a deep ruffle at the neckline to ruffles where the sleeves ended at her elbows to the waterfall of ruffles down the skirt. The flounces were made of a thinner fabric than the skirt so that they shimmered and danced with every movement. Like sunbeams, I thought. The dress was very beautiful, but Princess Mariposa was even more beautiful. She smiled at me and I felt my cheeks grow warm.

"Please, Your Highness," Lindy said, puffing with effort. "Stand still, just for a moment."

"It was the most fun I've had all summer!" the Princess exclaimed.

"Dancing with Baron Raskolnikov?" Cherice asked, juggling gloves, a parasol, a lace shawl, and a pair of silk slippers.

"No," the Princess said, giggling, "getting that impoverished prince to talk."

"I can't see the fun in that," Lindy groused, tugging on an uncooperative layer of petticoat. "Men who won't talk don't sound too interesting."

"How rude of him," Cherice said, clicking her tongue.

"Oh," Princess Mariposa replied, "he was ever so polite. He talked, just not about himself."

"What did he talk about, then?" Cherice asked.

Princess Mariposa sighed, her pretty black lashes fluttering like moths. "Prince Sterling—that's his name—talked about the stars, the seas, the wonders of the world."

"Humph," Lindy muttered. "There, that should do it." She spotted me and signaled for the handkerchief.

I clutched the warm handkerchief, reluctant to let it go. Lindy motioned again, mouthing, *Hurry up.*

"Much better," Princess Mariposa said, smoothing her ruffled waist. "But where is my hank—*There* it is!" She reached out to me.

Out of the corner of my eye, I saw Lindy turn a dull purple. Ignoring her, I stepped up, agog at the trembling ruffles, and handed Princess Mariposa her handkerchief. She took it in a waft of rose-scented air. I inhaled. Princesses smelled heavenly.

"It's still warm," Princess Mariposa cooed, and placed the handkerchief against her cheek. "It reminds me of when I was little and Nurse would put a warm pillowcase on my pillow on cold nights."

"That sounds nice," I said, forgetting that I was merely an Under-presser.

"Very nice," Princess Mariposa said, her sea-blue eyes alight. "And you are?"

"Darling Dimple," I said. And then I curtsied. Just like a fine lady.

The Princess beamed. And I was sure she meant to say

something more, but Cherice interrupted her with a pair of slippers. Lindy shooed me toward the door. I took the smallest step backward.

"Your impoverished Prince Sterling sounds like a dreamer. Not the sort who could manage a kingdom," Cherice said.

The Princess laughed. "Wasn't it *you* who said that I should look for some good in these suitors?"

I took another baby step toward the door.

A flash of irritation crossed the Wardrobe Mistress's face, followed by a bright smile. "Indeed, my dear. It was me." She knelt down to help the Princess into her slippers. "And you *should* look for the good. Just be careful the good you see is goodness and not some lesser quality."

"Lesser quality?" Princess Mariposa paused to hold up her skirts and admire the orangey-gold slippers on her feet.

Lindy glowered at me. I took another step.

"Pride, for example, my dear," Cherice said, "often masquerades as goodness. If it's conversation you desire, I should think that handsome, clever Prince . . ." Her voice faded. She put a finger to her chin and wrinkled her brow in thought. "Prince, er, Prince—"

"Baltazar," Princess Mariposa supplied.

Cherice draped a lace shawl over the Princess's ruffle-covered shoulders. "Oh, yes, Prince Baltazar. What did he have to say for himself?"

Lindy lunged for me, grabbed my elbow, and hustled me to the door. She shoved me through and shut the pressing room door firmly behind us.

"Next time, stop at the door and hand *me* the hankie. Understand?" Lindy glared at me for a minute. I nodded. "Finish that basket of towels," she continued, pointing to a basket of bright white towels used by the Princess. "And then you can have the rest of the day off."

The rest of the day off—I skipped off to do the pressing as Lindy slipped over to the cupboard and fished out her cloak. I hardly noticed as she left. I whipped through the towels, careful to focus on each one. I'd *talked* to the Princess! I couldn't wait to tell Jane and Gillian . . . when they were finished working for the day. Which wouldn't be for hours and hours. I sighed as I folded a towel.

I had the rest of the afternoon off—what to do with it? I could sneak out to the stables and see what Roger was up to. I wrinkled my nose. No boy would appreciate my grand conversation with the Princess. Why, she and I were practically best friends already. He was sure not to understand. Boys didn't understand much beside shovels and horses.

The Cooks, the Gardeners, and the Guards would all be busy with their duties. None of them would have time to listen to me. I set the last crisply ironed, bright white, scorch-free towel on the stack and dampened the stove.

I refilled my water bottle, smoothed down my apron, and went to see what Cherice was doing. Maybe she needed a little help sorting out ball gowns.

The wardrobe hall was dark, the candles blown out, and the massive books closed. Obviously Cherice had more interesting plans than talking to me. I twisted the handles on the closets—just to be sure that they were locked. I chewed my lower lip. A whole closet packed full of ball gowns—fabulously jeweled ball gowns—was just out of my reach. Why, if I could just get in there, I could daydream the day away.

The faintest *cheep-cheep* tickled my ears. That's when it came to me: the canary needed company. I needed company. All those hundred dresses—they needed someone to give them a good trying-on. And I was just the girl to help them out.

8

I eased open the door to Queen Candace's closet. Sunlight slid over my boots and painted my white pinafore gold. The canary perked up and sang. And the hundred dresses quivered with delight—as if they knew what they were waiting for. I shut the door behind me. No one had told me I couldn't try on these dresses. But then again, no one had said I could either.

"Which one should I try on first?" I asked the canary. He bobbed on his little gold swing and whistled. "You'll signal me?" I asked, grinning. The canary hopped up and down.

All right, then. The first hanger held a dark aqua satin gown with gold-trimmed sleeves and a skirt so full, you could run it up a mast and sail away. I spread the skirt with my hands, yards and yards of it, cool and thick and . . . The canary cocked his head as though waiting for me to move on. At the second hanger, the canary blinked at me as if to hurry me up. So I ran my hand along the tops of the hangers. At Eleven, the canary warbled merrily.

I frowned. With so many very beautiful dresses, Eleven wasn't my first choice. It wasn't ugly . . . exactly. It was sewn of tissue-thin silver cloth, edged with silver-gilt ribbons, and embroidered with silver-gilt flowers around the neckline. It was elegant but simple. No flashing rubies, no golden sashes, no . . . sparkle, just a soft silver glow. I slid my hand to hanger twelve and the canary shrieked.

I snatched my hand away.

"All right, don't be testy," I scolded the cheeky canary.

I went back to Eleven. At my touch, the gown poured off the hanger and into my hands. It felt impossibly light and soft, as though it were sewn from clouds. I held it up to my shoulders and it fell down, pooling around my feet. The gown had been made for a full-sized lady, not a slightly-tall-for-her-age eleven-year-old girl with dandelion fluff hair. I shrugged and undid the laces. I would just pretend to be full-sized, a queen like Candace. I stepped into the skirt and pulled the bodice up over my own clothes. I was the Queen of the Mist, stepping down from the clouds to grant little canaries their fondest wishes.

The shoulders were too wide for me, the skirt dragged

on the floor, and the sleeves hung over my hands. I saw myself reflected in the window; the soft silver glow of the gown lit my dandelion hair like candlelight. My face glowed. I pulled the sleeves back; my hands shone. The canary warbled his approval. And the dress sighed—really, I'm telling you, the dress let out a sigh of relief—and wiggled, jerked, and then—

The bodice hugged me. The sleeves slipped up to my wrists. The skirt rose to the top of my toes. In an instant, the dress was exactly my size. I blinked at my reflection. I was . . . a fairy standing on a rose petal, glistening like the dew, and radiant with fairy dust. I twirled. The skirt flew around my knees in a silver spiral. I could dance on the point of a pin, a tiny sprite. I dipped and swayed and spun—and spilled to a stop as I caught a glimpse of the doorway.

The Supreme Scrubstress stood there. Right smack-dab in the middle of the door to Queen Candace's closet. I threw my hands to my cheeks and screamed.

At the same moment, the Supreme Scrubstress screamed. I screamed again and so did she. We stood staring at each other, red-faced with guilt, hands to our cheeks. I slowly lowered mine and she did hers.

"May I help you?" I asked, uncertain whether or not it would be a good idea to explain what I was doing dressed in Queen Candace's gown.

"May I help you?" the Supreme Scrubstress mouthed at the same time.

"Um?" I said.

"Um," she mimicked.

I scratched my forehead. She scratched hers. Ooh, she was mocking me! I planted my fist on my hip, ready to give her a piece of my mind. (I'd noticed she hadn't brought along her gigantic wooden-handled sponge and therefore couldn't swat me with it.) She planted her fist. I pointed a finger at her. She pointed one at me.

"I work for Lindy now," I told her. "You're not my boss anymore!"

She mouthed the same words back at me. My forehead wrinkled up. Why couldn't I hear her? Was she whispering? I hadn't lost my hearing, because I could hear myself just fine. So what was going on?

That's when I remembered that I had closed the door when I came in.

The Supreme Scrubstress was standing in midair . . . floating in a mirror fixed to the back of the door. Which was impossible. I crept up to the mirror and touched the glass. The tips of our fingers met.

"You're not really there," I told her. "This is a trick." I looked over my shoulder and saw my reflection in the window looking over my silver-gowned shoulder at me. I glanced back at the Supreme Scrubstress in the mirror. I slid the gown off and let it fall around my waist.

There I stood reflected in the mirror, a dandelion-fluff-haired girl in a silver-gray dress and a white apron with a wad of silver fabric around her middle. I pulled the dress back up and snap, the gown whipped around me, perfectly sized, and there in the mirror was the Supreme Scrubstress.

"Is this why you wanted me to try on this dress? So I could look like . . . Marci?" I asked the canary.

He developed a sudden interest in preening his feathers and wouldn't meet my eye. I pulled the dress off and stepped out of it. It sighed again. *Seriously.* I held it firmly to show it who was boss and marched it back to its hanger.

"You're a very nice dress, Eleven, and I'm sure there is someone who would love to wear you and look like Marci, but that someone isn't me." I hung it up and gave a little pat, to show it there were no hard feelings on my part.

But I shuddered on the inside. Of all the people I might want to look like, the Supreme Scrubstress was *not* on my list. If I had to iron a stack of rags as high as the highest tower in the castle, I wouldn't miss working for her. Not for a minute. Why, just seeing her in the doorway had nearly whacked me sideways.

I sidled toward the door, having had enough excitement

for one day. The canary's head popped up. I waved. "Bye," I called as I whipped open the closet door and skirted through. I shut the door on the canary's outburst of protest and leaned against it, feeling wrung out like a dishrag.

I wondered what Roger was up to in the nice, safe, quiet stable.

9

I skipped into the yard. Roger would be working, but most stable jobs allowed for some talking. If he was shoveling something nasty, I would hold my nose while I talked. I found Roger on a bench polishing the silverwork on a bridle.

"Hey, Roger," I said, smoothing my crisp white apron.

Roger ducked his head, rubbing harder with his cloth. A nasty grease stain darkened the crown of his green cap; his freckles vanished in the shadow cast by the brim. "I figured you'd forget us living up there where the servants sit all day so that their clothes ain't mussed."

"I wish." I snorted. "*We* never sit down."

"Regular tyrant that Mariposa, I hear," Roger said.

"She is not!" I punched him in the shoulder. Hard. "You take that back."

He pulled off his cap and ran a hand through his sandy hair. He looked me up and down, from my new gray boots to the wisps of dandelion-fluff hair working free of my silver-gray ribbon.

"I take it back," he said, then laid his cap aside and went back to work. "Gillian's lost without your stories. Her Supreme Scrubself has been making everyone's life a misery."

"Oh." I sank onto the bench next to him. I'd missed everyone, but it hadn't occurred to me that they'd miss me too. Well, except for Jane, and she *had* to miss me. I was almost her real daughter.

"I didn't ask for it," I said.

"No, but you didn't beg to stay."

"Would you beg to stay in the under-cellar?"

"Nope."

"Well then . . ." I picked up his cap and studied the stain, which reminded me of an ostrich wearing a hair bow.

"Like it up there?"

"The Princess is very kind. But my boss, Lindy, has the temper of a Laundress who's dropped her soap in the sawdust." I chuckled, picturing Lindy scrubbing clothes. "I bet those Laundresses can get that stain out of your cap."

"Said it would cost me; not their regular job to clean caps."

"Oh. How much?"

"Enough. I ain't got it either way."

I frowned. I didn't have any pocket money myself. Princess's Girls worked for room and board. So did Stable Boys. You had to get promoted up another step from where we were to get pay. The Head Steward called it starting at the bottom. He wasn't kidding.

"You make new friends?" Roger asked in a too-casual tone.

I squinted at him. If Gillian missed me, did that mean that he did too? He polished away without looking up.

"Francesca, the Head Girl, hates me. She dumps sand in my bed every night so that she can make me sweep it up every morning," I admitted. "The other girls follow her lead."

"Figures."

"Why?" I asked. "Why should it figure?"

"You got her sister's job is why it figures." Roger gave the silver a last buff and held it up to the sunlight. "Perfect."

"Sister's job?" I said, confused. "I got the last Under-presser's job because she—she . . ."

"Got sacked by the Princess," Roger said. "Didn't you know? Faustine is Francesca's sister. Their mother is the

Head Housekeeper and she has big ambitions for those two. Thought they'd run the castle one day. *You* ruined that."

I folded my arms across my chest and sat back against the stable wall. I didn't know Mrs. Pepperwhistle, the Head Housekeeper. I'd seen her, of course, but she ruled the Upper-servants. Our paths hadn't crossed in the under-cellar. "Huh. That makes sense. Not that it's fair. It's stupid. I didn't ask for Faustine's job."

"Well, you got it."

For a moment, I was tempted to tell Roger about the mice, the canary, and Eleven. But then he stood up and ruined everything.

"It's your fault you got it," he said.

I jumped up and hurled his cap at him. He caught it with one hand. "What do you mean *my* fault?" I demanded, planting a fist on my hip.

"If it weren't for your daydreaming, the Supreme Scrub-stress would have sent those two to the Head Steward to get someone. And then you'd still be an Under-scrubber. And things would be the way they was supposed to." He parked his cap on his head and walked away.

I opened my mouth to yell at him, but nothing came out.

10

Stars sparkled in the purple night sky. The Underservants dotted the lower garden, sitting on benches and on patches of velvety grass enjoying the evening breeze. Light glowed in the castle windows, lending a soft luster to the gardens. I snuggled deeper into the cleft between the lion's bronze paws where I sat curled up next to Jane.

The lions guarded the garden's entrance, sending long shadows down the marble stairs and across the lawn. Sitting at their paws was almost like perching on the Princess's throne. It made my chest swell to have that top spot.

But tonight, I couldn't get Roger's words out of my mind. *And things would be the way they was supposed to.* Was I supposed to be an Under-scrubber stuck in the dark old under-cellar? Why couldn't I be an Upper-servant and live in the sunshine and be almost-friends with the Princess? I might daydream and tell stories, but I did my work.

I glanced at Jane. She wore a pinched expression, one that narrowed her blue eyes and wrinkled her pink cheeks. But she didn't look cross like the Supreme Scrubstress. Jane looked like a lady squinting at the world around her, uncertain what was what. She found a paper once that someone had spilled water on so that the colors ran together. She told me that was the way the world looked to her. I'd studied the blurry paper, but she kissed me and told me not to worry over it. As long as she could see sunlight, she was fine.

Jane sighed. And all the ladies around us sighed too, except Gillian, who coughed.

"How many closets?" she asked, reminding me where I'd left off describing the upper regions. "Six?"

"Seven, actually," a voice said.

I jumped in my seat. The Supreme Scrubstress lurked in the lion's shadow on the other side of Gillian. I hadn't heard her sit down, but I'd know that voice anywhere.

"Seven?" Gillian said, as if seven were a million.

I swallowed. "Yes, six for the Princess's clothes; there's a seventh, for old stuff."

The Supreme Scrubstress's eyes glinted in the dimness. I had the creepy feeling she knew I'd been in Queen Candace's closet. I wriggled, suddenly uncomfortable on the marble step.

"My grandmother served Queen Paloma, Mariposa's mother, as Wardrobe Mistress," the Supreme Scrubstress said.

This was news. I tried to picture the Supreme Scrubstress as a little girl . . . and failed.

"I spent hours watching her care for the Queen's clothes."

She spoke as if she knew things, things I'd like to know. The image of her in the mirror rose in my thoughts. Why did the canary want me to try on *that* dress?

"Did Queen Paloma have a canary?" I blurted out.

"Yes. A cute fellow; he'd belonged to Queen Candace," the Supreme Scrubstress replied.

"The closets?" Gillian said, tugging on my sleeve.

"Queen Candace?" I asked, sure I'd heard wrong.

"I remember that," Jane interrupted. "When I was a girl, the Head Cook said it was a magic canary that was passed from one Queen to the next."

The Cooks, Pickers, and other Under-servants snorted with laughter. I didn't laugh. I rubbed my nose, thinking hard. There *was* something odd about that bird.

"That's nothing," the Supreme Scrubstress said, and

waved her hand. "My grandmother told me how the castle was built. She was a child, ten or eleven then, and remembered it clearly."

"Oh, not the dragons," groaned a nearly bald Picker named Agnes.

"Dragons?" Gillian and I echoed, perking up.

"The castle *was* built by dragons," the Supreme Scrubstress said, poking her finger at Agnes.

"I haven't heard that story," I said.

"Me neither!" Gillian exclaimed.

"Oh, go on, tell it," a Cook said.

The Supreme Scrubstress smoothed her apron over her plump knees. "When Richard was King, a pair of dragons settled in the mountains above the castle. They snatched sheep and burned down cottages. They stole anything gold or silver. People were afraid—always keeping one eye on the horizon and one on the task at hand. Crops suffered from neglect. And herds dwindled. The people cried out to King Richard for help."

"Did he rescue them?" Gillian asked, twisting her apron.

The Supreme Scrubstress glared at her. "Don't interrupt. As I was saying, now Richard was a great king, a learned man, who traveled far and wide. He had just returned from some of his travels when he learned of the dragons. At once, he sent his best Archers to the castle towers to shoot down the dragons."

"Not his worst," Agnes murmured.

A chuckle ran through the group.

"I'd have marched out to fight them," a Footman boasted.

"King Richard realized that fighting fire-breathing dragons from the ground would result in a great loss of men," the Supreme Scrubstress snapped, quelling them with a glance. "Where was I? Oh, yes, but dragons fly very high and very fast, and the Archers couldn't bring them down. Instead, the arrows infuriated the dragons, and they set the castle aflame, burning it to the ground."

"So the King and a group of handpicked men scaled the mountain and cornered the dragons in their aerie. There they were, hunkered down on their treasure, unwilling to blast the King and risk melting all that lovely gold."

"Did he kill them?" Gillian whispered.

"No. Richard had, in his travels, collected unusual beasts for his menagerie, and the dragons were magnificent creatures. He hated to slay them. However, he didn't trust them. Once they'd been spared, what would keep them from resuming their destruction? So Richard had brought along beautiful golden collars. Because what dragon can resist anything shiny? Now, these were no ordinary collars. Once the dragons allowed the collars to be fastened around their necks, they fell under an enchantment, slaves as long as the collars held.

"King Richard ordered the dragons to build a castle to replace the one they'd destroyed. The dragons soared up the mountainside clutching massive blocks in their talons. Stone by stone, the castle rose. The people in the valley below gathered to watch.

"When the dragons finished building the new castle, they perched on the north tower to rest. King Richard sent his men to climb out on the roof, creep up on the dragons, and shackle them with great iron chains to the tower's spire. The captive dragons' cries echoed through the mountains, splintering stones and cracking evergreens. As the days passed, the cries quieted, and slowly but surely, the dragons hardened and turned to stone."

"Bah," Agnes said. "Where'd Richard find them collars?"

"Grandmother didn't know that; I asked," the Supreme Scrubstress replied. "Perhaps he found them on his travels."

"Ain't seen no menagerie," an Under-laundress scoffed.

"Oh? Then you've not taken a good look at the greenhouses," the Supreme Scrubstress retorted. "They were converted years ago."

I squinted; the greenhouses did resemble glass cages—a little.

"Dragons on the roof?" Gillian exploded. "There can't be!"

"Ask Jane," the Supreme Scrubstress said, folding her arms across her plump chest.

"Have you seen them, Jane?" I asked, tugging her sleeve.

Jane frowned. "What, dear?"

"Have you seen them? The dragons, I mean," I asked.

Worry marks creased the corners of Jane's eyes. She dabbed at her forehead with her handkerchief, stalling, I knew. She always stalled when I asked a question she didn't want to answer.

"My, but it is getting late," Jane said.

"Come on, tell them what a daredevil you were, how you walked the crossbeam on the north wing and saw them." The Supreme Scrubstress reached over us to poke Jane.

"You promised you would never tell that!" Jane said.

"At our age, I doubt anyone's going to send us to bed without our supper," she replied.

"Oh, please! Tell me!" I begged Jane, wringing her arm.

Remember how Jane had a soft spot for me the size of a plum pie? She must have misplaced it that evening, because she stood up.

"Time for bed!" she announced. She marched blindly down the stairs, scattering servants right and left as she went.

Magical canaries? Dragons on the roof? Mice who swept floors? Just what sort of a castle had I been living in for eleven years? Why hadn't Jane told me about the canary and the dragons? And what *else* hadn't she told me?

11

The next morning the sun sparkled on the sand-free floor. Francesca glared at me while I tied my pinafore and laced my boots. The other girls brushed past me with puzzled frowns. They all acted as though I had waved a wand and, *poof*, made the sand disappear. I grinned at the thought.

After they all left, I slipped a slice of cheese I'd kept from supper under my bed. A tiny, whiskered white nose peeked out from under the eiderdown. A pair of black eyes blinked solemnly at me. "Enjoy," I told him, and scurried off to work.

I arrived just in time to have a basket of sheets thrust at me.

"From now on, you press the Princess's sheets, towels,

and handkerchiefs. *I* see to the Princess's clothes. Understand?" Lindy said.

"Yes, ma'am," I crowed. I was an Upper-servant, one of the Princess's own Girls. I kicked the basket of practice rags aside and set the new one in its place.

"Mind you don't scorch anything!" Lindy called after me.

I pulled a sheet out of the basket, a rippling, glossy-white cloth as fine as a spider's web. My heart fluttered; this delicate fabric would be all too easy to scorch. I shook myself. Now was not the time to have doubts, not now that I'd graduated from practice rags. I set to work.

At first, it was easy. The wrinkles dissolved under my iron. But after a while, the sheets lost their sheen and simply became cloth. Acres and acres of white cloth. How large was the Princess's bed anyway? I parked my iron. Lindy had mentioned towels and handkerchiefs. I spied two more baskets waiting for me. Lindy was nowhere to be seen.

I ran a hand through my hair while my thoughts inched toward Queen Candace's closet. Had that canary really belonged to Queen Paloma, and Queen Candace before her? How old must he be? The Supreme Scrubstress had claimed the canary was magical. This might make sense if I believed in magical canaries, which I did not.

Did I?

I scratched my nose. That canary knew about Eleven. *That* dress was peculiar. Dresses remained on hangers until you wore them. The same as the sheets I'd pressed would sit in the basket until someone put them away in the cupboards. Sheets didn't spread themselves on beds any more than dresses sprang off hangers and dressed themselves on people. They stayed where you put them. They didn't *want* to be worn.

Did they?

I yanked my thoughts back to the remaining baskets of laundry. I ironed my way through the towels. Then I stared at the basket brimful of handkerchiefs; how many of these could one princess use? I glanced at the pile of freshly pressed and folded towels and sheets, each monogrammed with a silvery-gray *M*. How many days of laundry did this represent? Had Lindy been saving this for me to do? Or was this one day's worth?

I shook that thought right out of my head. I was the Under-presser; my job was to press the Princess's sheets, towels, and handkerchiefs. Princess Mariposa could use a hundred handkerchiefs a day if she wanted to. She was the Princess.

A whistle rippled through the room as if in agreement. That canary! What could he want now? I set my hot iron down on the stove and went to see. I poked my head into Queen Candace's closet. The canary greeted me with a song. Sunlight painted the glass canary in the window and scattered golden beams across the rose-strewn carpet. Everything seemed fine to me.

"I will feed you later," I told him. "I have a pile of ironing to do."

The silver hangers clattered on the closet rods.

"You're just a bunch of old dresses," I said aloud. Not to the dresses or to the canary. Not really. I said it out loud so that I could hear it.

The dresses roiled like a stewpot full of onions stirred by a spoon.

What had gotten into them?

"Oh, really," I began, and then I saw Eleven hanging limply on its hanger.

"Well, I'm sorry, but I did try you on once," I told it. "Once ought to suit anyone."

Eleven hung there like a damp towel. The other dresses quivered like the Supreme Scrubstress's outraged chins. With a loud sigh, I stalked into the closet, shut the door behind me, and plucked Eleven from the hanger.

"A quick try-on, that's it!" I told it with a shake. I pulled it on and turned to the mirror.

And there I was, Darling Dimple looking silly in a too-big, too-long silvery dress. No zip and the dress fit—and no Supreme Scrubstress. Eleven was . . . cloth, thread, ribbons, and buttons, nothing more. I turned to the canary, who blinked at me in an owlish manner.

"Well?" I said with my hand on my silver-clothed hip. "What's wrong now?"

The canary eyed me with his beady little eyes. I stared back. And then I decided that enough was enough. I took the dress off and put it back on the hanger where it belonged. A plum-colored ribbon curled around my wrist and tugged at me.

"I am very busy," I said, following the ribbon to Number Eighteen. Eighteen was a cream-colored silk with plum ribbons and sparkling diamond buttons. "You're very pretty, but I have so much—" Eighteen wrapped a sleeve around my waist and hugged me. "I can't try you all on. I have work to do."

I set about untangling myself from the sleeve and then a thought popped into my head. Who would I look like in this dress? The Supreme Scrubstress, me, or someone else?

My head buzzed. My heart pounded. Was *that* what the dresses were trying to tell me? That I could try them on and look like someone else? It had worked with Eleven. It didn't work now, but it had. Once. Yesterday. Holding my breath, I eased Eighteen off its hanger and stepped into it. Eighteen shivered delightedly and snuggled me up tight.

Once again, a perfect fit. I glanced at the mirror on the back of the door—and saw a beautiful lady with raven-colored curls tied back in a satin bow.

It *was* what the dresses were trying to tell me! Each dress worked once.

I grinned and the beautiful lady grinned with me. I wrinkled my/her porcelain nose in the mirror. I batted my/her dusky eyelashes over my/her sapphire eyes.

"Oh my, she's gorgeous!" I told the canary, who chose that moment to examine his little claws. "And look at her dress," I commanded, pointing. "Have you ever seen anything like it?" Because the dress in the mirror was not cream-colored silk; it was a bright turquoise embroidered all over with gold and crystals.

The canary didn't answer, so I turned back to the mirror. Who was she—the lady in the mirror? A princess? Or an enchantress from a faraway land? I shivered, thrilled at the thought. If Gillian could see this, she'd be so jealous her curls would kink right up into knots so tight they'd never comb out! I sashayed from side to side, setting the crystals twinkling. This lady must be a famous dancer who whirled around on the tips of her toes. I wouldn't mind looking like her all the time.

"Much better than Eleven," I murmured.

I clapped a hand over my mouth, suddenly aware that

the dresses were listening. I removed my hand and inhaled to apologize, and smelled something burning—

With a screech, I yanked open the door and raced to my ironing board. All three irons sizzled on the stove, glowing red-hot. Wisps of smoke hissed from their plates. A handkerchief sat close by, curling in the heat. I snatched the handkerchief away, fanning the air. My heart skipped twice. My knees felt watery. I mopped my brow with the handkerchief. What a close call! Another minute and something might have caught fire. I felt faint at the idea.

Sweat trickled down my neck. I dabbed at it with the soggy ball of handkerchief. Goodness! My eyes snapped open. In my clenched fist I held a grimy, wet handkerchief with a silvery-gray *M* embroidered on the corner. I gulped. I had used one of Princess Mariposa's own handkerchiefs! One of the delicate sparkly-clean handkerchiefs she touched to her own face.

Lindy would kill me.

The door to the hall swung open and one of Princess Mariposa's ladies came in. "There you are!" she said. "I've searched everywhere for you. The Princess is waiting!"

Princess Mariposa wanted me?

"Teresa!" the lady said, shaking my arm.

Teresa?

The lady snatched the handkerchief from my hand,

tossed it in a basket, and latched on to my wrist. "Come along," she said, and began dragging me to the door. At that moment, a second lady appeared.

"Oh, good, you found her. The Princess insists that Teresa sit next to her at lunch," the second lady said. "It was no use hiding, Teresa! It will be fine. The Princess won't bite you."

And with that, the two ladies marched me out of the pressing room.

12

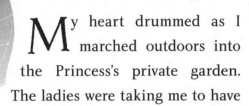

My heart drummed as I marched outdoors into the Princess's private garden. The ladies were taking me to have lunch with Princess Mariposa! I had to resist the urge to skip. I, Darling—no, wait, I, *Teresa*, had received an invitation to dine with the great, the beautiful, the . . . *legendary* Princess Mariposa. At my feet, a stone path led to a set of marble steps flanked by two marble peacocks. One of the ladies gave me a little push in the center of my back. I stumbled forward. She shooed me on with her hands.

"Down the stairs, first arch on the right, hurry," she hissed.

A part of me wanted to race down the steps and jump through the rose-covered arch. Another part of me wanted to rip Eighteen off and gallop back to the upper-attic before the real Teresa showed up and I got caught. Damp spots grew under my arms. I took a step down the stairs.

"Teresa," the other lady said, "the Princess is waiting."

"But I'm not really—"

The first lady wagged her finger at me. "Lady Teresa, if you don't go, your mother will have to be told! I'll write to her myself."

I frowned. Teresa was getting herself into quite a pickle here. Well, not here, because she wasn't here. I was. But she was getting herself into trouble wherever she was hiding.

"Please, Teresa," the second lady said.

I swallowed hard. I should have told them I wasn't Teresa right away. Now it was too late. I would have to go to lunch and be Teresa. I glanced down at Eighteen. How long did the magic last? What if Eighteen dozed off or whatever magic dresses did, and Princess Mariposa saw me instead of Teresa? How would I explain? "I'm sorry, Your Highness, but the dress made me try it on"?

The worst thing that could happen to Eighteen was to be sent back to its hanger. The worst thing that could happen to me was—I didn't want to imagine what the worst thing might be. I'd have to go have lunch with Princess Mariposa and hope that the real Teresa stayed hidden. And that Eighteen behaved.

I walked down the steps and along the path.

"You wanted me to put you on. You're in this with me. If I get caught, you get caught," I scolded Eighteen under my breath. The waistband squeezed me. The dress had heard.

"All right, then," I murmured.

First arch on the right. With a deep gulp, I plunged through the arch.

The clink of silverware greeted me, along with a murmur of conversation and the Princess's warm laughter. Lunch had already been served. I *was* late. Princess Mariposa presided over a table crowded with guests and nestled under a golden canopy. A blond-haired man with huge shoulders sat at the Princess's right side. The seat on her left was vacant. She waved at me with a silver soupspoon, eyes twinkling.

"Here she is!" Princess Mariposa announced.

Everyone turned to stare at me. A blush bloomed on my cheeks. I wrinkled Eighteen in my sweaty hands. What would the real Teresa do if she were here? What would she say to them? What would *I* say? *My, what a lot of handkerchiefs Your Highness uses.*

"We saved you a chair." Princess Mariposa patted the seat beside her.

There was nothing else to do but sit in the chair the Princess was saving for Teresa. Princess Mariposa squeezed my hand under the table.

"I am famished! Let's finish our soup!"

Everyone picked up their spoons. The portly gentleman across the table nodded to me.

"Tomato and basil," he offered. "Excellent." His bowl was nearly empty.

The blond man leaned closer to the Princess. "As I was saying, Your Highness, my last hunt was quite . . . exhilarating." He flashed a smile at the Princess and leaned a little closer.

I took a sip of my soup, thankful that someone else was talking and I didn't have to. The soup *was* excellent, rich and creamy. I scooped up another, bigger bite.

"Good?" the portly gentleman asked.

"Excellent," I said, echoing his opinion.

He smiled at me as if I'd passed some difficult test.

A gloved hand reached in front of me and plucked up my bowl. Startled, I turned in my seat. A Footman stood behind me, collecting soup bowls and setting them on the tray he carried. I waved, hoping he would bring back my uneaten soup, but he kept walking. With a sigh, I turned back around. This was the shortest, smallest lunch I'd had in ages. Frowning, I wondered how poor Princess Mariposa lasted until evening on only a bowl of soup.

"That's just the first course," a voice beside me said.

The gentleman who sat next to me wasn't as big or broad-shouldered as the man on Princess Mariposa's other side, but he had warm brown eyes and a kind smile. He dusted his hand off on his faded brocade coat and offered it to me.

"Prince Sterling," he said. "And you are the mysteriously always-absent Teresa. Pleased to meet you."

Prince Sterling! The impoverished prince that I'd overhead Princess Mariposa talking about, the one she'd so enjoyed talking to. I beamed.

I shook his hand. "Pleased to meet you," I said, hoping that was what the mysteriously absent Teresa would say.

A quizzical look lightened Prince Sterling's eyes. He squeezed my fingers and glanced down at my hand. It looked like a grown-up lady's hand, but maybe it didn't feel like one. I snatched it back and tucked it safely under the table.

"What's the second course?" I asked, stomach rumbling.

He looked puzzled for a moment. Then his smile returned. "Spinach salad," he said, darting his eyes at a glossy paper card by my plate.

I picked it up. It read, MENU FOR MARIPOSA'S RUBY LUNCHEON, followed by twelve lines of curly writing. Oh. A blush crept up my cheeks. A similar card was parked by each plate. Everyone else at the table knew enough to read the menu. Everyone but me. Well, this *was* my first lunch with a princess. I skimmed the long list. Spinach salad

91

with strawberries, pickled beets à l'orange, red snapper with dill sauce, shrimp paella, roasted red peppers, and brandied cherries, just for starters. I gulped. Who could eat all that for lunch?

"The menu tells you what will be served for each course. That way you can save room for your favorites," Prince Sterling whispered, glancing at the portly gentleman, "and not have to be carried away from the table on a stretcher."

I giggled. I could picture the portly gentleman bursting his seams as an overworked Footman staggered under his weight. The portly gentleman glowered as if he could read my mind.

The gloved hand of a Footman set a plate of spinach salad before me. I reached for my fork and found four of them lined up by my plate. Prince Sterling winked and picked up the fork farthest from his plate. So I copied him. Course after course appeared before me and course after course was whisked away. I ate only a few bites of each. The portly gentleman scraped every plate clean. I watched him eat, eyes wide. As another forkful disappeared into his mouth, I imagined a *thud* echoing through the cavern of his ironclad stomach.

Princess Mariposa picked at her food while the blond gentleman talked. And talked. Occasionally a few words filtered my way. "A close corner, Your Highness." "We climbed undaunted by the wind." "A long shot, but I knew we had to take it."

Princess Mariposa murmured polite responses until the man said, "The largest *Lycaena alciphron* I've ever seen." At that, her eyes snapped open wide. "Oh, Prince Baltazar, you saw one!"

I blinked. A Lycany alicpropro, er what?

"This big," Prince Baltazar said, spreading his fingers two inches apart. Which didn't seem very big to me, but Princess Mariposa gasped.

"Really?" she breathed.

Prince Baltazar smiled, revealing all his gleaming white teeth. "Really. And I thought you might like to see it." He produced a small glass-lidded wooden box from his jacket and offered it to the Princess. "For you, my sweet Mariposa. Note the sapphire-burnished body, the rich copper wings, the velvety black spots, and the whisker-thin antennae."

"A *Lycaena alciphron*," Princess Mariposa said, cradling the box in her palm and gazing at it with rapture. "It's so beautiful."

"It barely holds a candle to your luster, my dear," Prince Baltazar said.

I craned my neck to see inside the box. A small brightly colored butterfly lay pinned to the box's bottom. I cringed at the sight of the sharp silver pins.

"It's known as a purple-shot copper," Prince Sterling whispered in my ear. "Rather rare and hard to catch, but much prettier flying free."

I nodded. I pictured the tiny creature fluttering over a field of flowers. Poor little butterfly, caught and pinned. A tear trembled on my eyelash.

"Teresa, don't cry," Princess Mariposa said.

"I—I'm not." I dashed the tear away and smiled my best fake-Teresa smile. But a second tear trickled down my cheek.

Princess Mariposa bit her lower lip. She turned to Prince Baltazar. "Thank you very much; I shall add this to my collection." She signaled a Footman, who placed the box on a tray and bore it away. Then she tossed her napkin on the table and rose.

Everyone at the table rose with her. I lurched to my feet.

"No, no," Princess Mariposa said. "I insist that all of you stay and enjoy the remainder of my Ruby Luncheon. Teresa, will you accompany me inside?"

"Yes," I said with a regretful glance at the raspberry ice melting in a silver dish.

The Princess took my arm and we walked away across the lawn. My face flushed—we were alone, she and I. Would she ask me questions I couldn't answer? I wished with all my might that the real Teresa would appear and rescue me.

"I'm so sorry about your mother's illness. You've only just arrived and now—so very soon—you must return home," Princess Mariposa said. Her sea-blue eyes darkened.

Oh, poor Teresa. She must have been too worried to come to lunch.

Princess Mariposa gave my arm a gentle squeeze. "Promise you'll come again. I know you don't like strangers and all this fuss," she said, whisking them away with a wave of her hand. "But I've so wanted to get to know you better." A shadow passed over the Princess's face as if some sadness weighed on her. "I hope, Cousin, that we can be friends."

"Me too," I said.

Princess Mariposa smiled, aglow with the same delight with which she'd viewed the *Lycaena alciphron*. "We could be sisters."

"Sisters," I echoed.

Sisters. What would it be like to have Princess Mariposa as a sister? To be Princess Darling? I'd wear a great lot of beautiful clothes and eat Ruby Luncheons every day. And I'd have an army of servants at my beck and call.

"Up here," Princess Mariposa said, gesturing to a set of stone stairs.

I blinked. I had no idea where in the gardens we were. Servants like me weren't allowed anywhere the Princess walked. At the top of the stairs Princess Mariposa stopped. We stood on a terrace of pale bricks that shimmered as if a sprite had sprinkled fairy dust over them. The bricks radiated from a starburst in the center of the terrace. Along the outer edge, at each star point, stood a bronze deer on a pedestal. Across the patio the castle walls rose in gleaming white tiers. From here, I could see the stone gryphons guarding each tower and the eagles and falcons circling the barricades. Higher up, squinting hard, I could make out other birds, too far away to identify.

Which made me wonder, why decorate a castle with sculptures too small to be seen from the ground? Because looking up and down the castle, I couldn't see any place one could stand to see them. The only ones who had seen them were the original builders—who were dragons, if you believed the Supreme Scrubstress. I rubbed my eyes, tilted my head *waaaay* back, and craned my neck to see if I could see the dragons that she said were on the tallest spire.

I couldn't see a thing.

Princess Mariposa turned to me and said, "If there is anything you want to ask . . ."

Before I could stop myself I blurted out, "Was the castle really built by dragons? Are they really up there?"

Princess Mariposa blinked in surprise. And then

she laughed. "Has your mother told you those stories? I suppose she has. I'll tell you a secret. Come here." She squeezed my hand and walked me over to the starburst. "Stand in the center and look north," she whispered in my ear. "On a clear day, if you look hard enough, you can see them from this one spot."

She dropped my hand and stepped back. Holding my breath, I slid one foot onto the starburst and then the other. I lifted my skirt to see the pale bricks shining around my gray boots. *My gray boots!* I snatched my hand from my skirt. Here I was, Darling Dimple, Under-presser, learning a secret meant for the Princess's cousin Teresa. A guilty lump rose in my throat.

Princess Mariposa motioned impatiently for me to look north, toward the tall, silver-tipped white tower high in the center of the castle. I couldn't disappoint her. Well, and I really, *really* wanted to look and see these dragons for myself.

So I did.

I shaded my eyes with my hand and focused all my attention on that top tower. I spied the silver tip and traveled down the gleaming white side until I saw the plinth at the base. From there I traced the line of the crossbeam, the *fuzzy, bumpy line.* I gasped. The fuzziness solidified into the outline of a dragon curled up at the base of the tower.

Clapping a hand over my mouth to hold back a scream, I lost my balance and stepped off the starburst. The outline of the dragon vanished into the afternoon sunlight.

I stood, shaky, excited, and not a little frightened. I had seen one of the dragons! I really had. They were up there. They were real.

Princess Mariposa put an arm around my shoulders and squeezed. "Makes you think, doesn't it?"

"What if they got loose?" I asked. "What if they came down here?"

"They're shackled by a magic poured into gold collars. They can't come down; you're safe."

"Safe," I agreed. But I wondered how safe was safe. How did the magic get poured into those collars? What would happen if someone knew how to pull it out again? How safe would we all be then?

"What if someone tampered with them?" I said.

Princess Mariposa hugged me. "Oh, Teresa, don't worry. There is only one way to touch that magic, one talisman that can unlock it, and it is secure in the King's treasury."

"Oh," I said.

"Grandmother Candace told me so. She didn't say what it was, only that it was safe."

"But your father knew," I said, "right? He knew what it was."

She shook her head. "Grandmother died unexpectedly; she never told my father. However, do not worry; nothing has been removed from the regalia, so it is still there."

I imagined the King dressed in all his ceremony attire. Which piece was the talisman? Had Princess Mariposa ever gone looking for it? Could she guess what it might be? Or how it was used? Was it gold? Or cloth? Or silver? A crown or a robe or a ring or a scepter?

Princes Mariposa sighed. "You should go in now. They will have packed your things, and no doubt that coach is waiting."

I promised to come back and visit again. She bid me farewell with a kiss on my cheek and sent me on my way. As I went, I cast one last look at the tower. *Dragons on the roof!* I wished that canary could do more than sing. There was a thing or two I'd like to ask him.

If only the dresses could talk.

13

Spots swam before my eyes as I walked out of the sunshine and into the castle. I batted at them with my hand. I had never been on this side of the castle before. I had walked straight through the door Princess Mariposa had pointed to because that's what Teresa would have done. But I wasn't Teresa. I couldn't follow the Princess's instruction to turn left and go up the stairs to the west wing. *That* was the last thing I could do. Someone would pounce on me and stuff me into Teresa's coach. I would wind up who-knows-where wearing a dress that didn't belong to me and impersonating the Princess's cousin . . . who knew what would happen after that?

As the spots dissolved, the room took shape, a long gallery lined with paintings. Another day, I might have dawdled to look at the pictures, but I heard footsteps coming down the stairs. I galloped down the gallery, plunged through the far door, and ran *smack-dab* into a knot of ladies.

"Lady Teresa, they are waiting for you upstairs," one said.

Drat this Teresa! Why didn't she come out of hiding and deal with her own problems? Drat Eighteen! I had to get it off as soon as possible or my goose was surely cooked. I thought for a second. If I looked like Teresa, then I should get out of this by doing something the Princess's cousin would do. So I held my head high and replied in a cool voice.

"I am on an errand for Her Highness," I said.

I strolled across the room, round a bend, and up some stairs, then opened the first door I came to, taking my own sweet time on my "errand." I figured that if I acted like I knew what I was doing, they'd think I did. The room I entered was a bedroom with a bed piled high with puffy comforters. A tall wardrobe stood in the corner. I glanced around. There was nothing in the room to tell whether or not anyone was using it or who they might be. But it was empty at the moment.

I peeled Eighteen off my shoulders. The burgundy ribbons wrapped themselves around my waist, squeezing as I tried to push the dress below my waist.

"No, no," I told it. "I have to get you off before we get in trouble." The dress squeezed tighter. I was in a pickle. I had to get this thing off before someone came looking for Teresa. I didn't think I'd been followed, but I couldn't be sure. I shoved the dress down. I yanked on the hem. I wriggled and squirmed and the dress grew tighter.

Then I had an idea. "I—I can't breathe," I gasped. "I'm feeling dizzy. I—I—I think I might faint." I threw my hand to my forehead and swayed back and forth. Which must have made Eighteen nervous because it loosened just enough. I made a grab for it and wrestled the dress to my ankles, fighting free of the burgundy ribbons wrapped around my feet.

Then, panting from my struggle, I couldn't resist giving the dress a good shaking. Which would have made me feel better, but now the dress was just a dress, limp and lifeless. And I was just me, Darling Dimple, lost in a strange part of the castle. Holding a stolen dress. A dress that belonged to a Queen. Standing in a bedroom I had no business being in after I ate a lunch that wasn't meant for me and heard a secret I wasn't supposed to hear.

How did I get into this mess?

Tears started in my eyes. I reached into my pocket for a handkerchief and pulled out the folded-up map I'd drawn from the one in the pressing room. The map included only a small piece of the castle—the rooms where the Princess's Girls needed to be—but at each edge arrows pointed north, west, east, and south. Each arrow was labeled. And the west arrow was labeled west wing.

A huge grin curled my lips. "I have an idea," I told Eighteen. I couldn't walk through the castle holding the Queen's dress, but I could hide it here and come back for it tonight when everyone was asleep. I threw open the wardrobe—which was packed with linens. I folded the dress in as neatly as a long, silky, ribbon-dripping dress could be folded and slipped it between the sheets.

"Wait here," I told it. "I'll be back."

I closed the wardrobe, tiptoed over to the door, and inched it open. The corridor was clear—a corridor painted pale peach and lined with white doors. White plaster mice danced down strips of wainscoting decorating the walls. I chewed my lower lip; I had to find this same room again tonight, when everything would be dark. It wasn't like there was a big sign pointing the way for me: *here, Darling, this is the room!* Well, I could count how many doors this door was from the end of the hall. Running my fingers along the dancing mice, I counted as I went; three, four, five, six . . . up ahead I saw another peach-painted corridor. How many peach corridors were there in the west wing? How would I be sure I had the right one?

My finger hit a hole in the wainscoting and I stopped. There in plaster lay the outline of where mice ought to be but were missing—as if whoever did the plaster forgot to put them in. Five mice, one large mouse and four little ones, were gone from the wall as if they had jumped down and run away.

Where would five plaster mice go?

A chill shook me. I knew where those mice were. But how did they get out of the plaster and *why* were they living under my bed? I didn't think it was because they enjoyed sweeping my floor. There had to be another reason. But what? This was like some far-fetched adventure story.

If this was an adventure, I was the one having it.

I, Darling Dimple, was having an adventure. Or it was having me. I wasn't sure which. All I knew was that I hadn't finished my ironing, and I had no idea how long I'd been gone. A very *annoyed* Lindy would be waiting for me, Darling Dimple, ex-Presser . . . I had to get back as quickly as possible and save my job! I whipped around and counted the doors back from the missing mice to the bedroom. Those mice could help me find the corridor. I'd bribe them with my supper if I had to.

Heart pounding, I threaded my way back to my side of the castle, popping my map out of my pocket to check where I was. No one paid me any attention; now that I was me wearing the uniform of a Princess's Girl, I was almost invisible.

In the pressing room, Lindy was marching up and down before my ironing board, holding a wad of something up in the air, ranting.

"If this don't beat all," she said, stomping for emphasis. "The work these people do, the sloppy, no-good—I have half a mind to report this. The Princess ought to know what goes on around here!"

This was it; I was going to be fired and thrown out of the castle.

My knees knocked together so loudly Lindy heard them and whirled around. Her long hair snapped around her head like a slingshot. Her cheeks burned with anger. Her eyes boiled. I swear a wisp of steam rose off the top of her head. And in her hand was the soiled handkerchief I had used to wipe my face. The one the lady had tossed into one of the baskets. My heart rose into my throat and lodged behind my Adam's apple. Lindy shook the handkerchief at me.

"This! This is what the Laundress sent up!" she announced. "This filthy, smelly wad! What was she thinking?"

Lindy was mad at the Laundress, not me. I swallowed my heart back down into my chest.

"Well?" she asked as if she expected an answer.

"I—I don't know," I said, my voice coming out all scratchy.

"She ought to be boiled in her own vat! The idea that the Princess would accept *this*," she panted, shaking the handkerchief at me again.

The Head Laundress and all the Laundresses worked on the opposite side of the under-cellar from the Scrubbers. They all had been kind to me. The thought of one of them being punished for something that was my fault . . . well, it made me feel downright ill. I'd have to confess.

Just then Cherice swooped into the room, a whirl of ice-blue skirts.

"Oh, my dear, have you heard? The Princess is smitten. Smitten!" Cherice sang out. "That clever Baltazar has finally made some headway into her heart. How, you ask? Why, my dear, with a tiny little butterfly. Isn't that romantic? Love has wings, they say!"

Lindy glared, still steaming.

Cherice noticed the handkerchief. "What is this?" she asked.

"This is a flat-out dereliction of duty," Lindy answered.

Sweat trickled down my spine. I'd have to confess in front of both of them.

"A soiled handkerchief?" Cherice smiled.

"A soiled handkerchief stuffed in a basket of *my* pressing!"

"Oh," Cherice said. Then she teased the handkerchief

out from between Lindy's fingers. "This is a happy day. You mustn't let some little thing mar it. I am sure that this is nothing more than a very unfortunate, but honest, mistake. I will wash this myself. Nice as new. And I am sure Darling would be happy to press it, no?"

"No!" I exclaimed.

Both women turned to gape at me.

"Er, yes, I mean yes. I will press it up good as new," I said, pouncing on this opportunity to fix my mistake without admitting to it.

The red of Lindy's cheeks softened a shade. Her rigid shoulders relaxed a fraction.

Cherice took Lindy by the arm. "You could use a cup of tea, my dear."

Lindy took a step for the door. "Darlin', I see you didn't finish this morning."

I held my breath. This was it. Lindy was going to yell at me.

"I see you were being extra careful. That's good. But be sure and get all that done this afternoon."

I blinked, too stunned to speak. Lindy's eyebrow went up. I nodded vigorously.

"All right, then," she said. And the two of them went off to have their tea.

The breath went out of me in a slow whistle. I collapsed

into a heap on the floor. My job was safe. I hadn't gotten caught being Teresa. No one knew the dress was missing. I was safe.

Safe.

Safer than that butterfly Prince Baltazar had pinned to that box.

This reminded me of what Cherice had said about Prince Baltazar winning his way into the Princess's heart with a butterfly. I scratched my side. It hadn't seemed that way to me. She'd liked the butterfly, but had it won her heart? Princess Mariposa didn't strike me as the sort to be won so easily. It was a pretty butterfly, but it was also a dead butterfly. I chewed my lower lip. And Baltazar, he was tall and good-looking, but something about him nagged me. He didn't seem *fine* enough for my Princess.

I tried to conjure up the sort of prince who would be fine enough . . . and failed. I got up and fed the stove under my irons. It wasn't any of my business who the Princess fell in love with. But if I were her, I'd find someone really wonderful. Someone exciting . . . like her grandfather King Richard, who could chain dragons to the roof.

14

That night when I slid my hand between my bedsheets to scoop out the sand, there wasn't any there. I felt all over inside my covers. No sand. I checked under my pillow. Nothing. I peeked under my bed. The dim shape of my box stamped ARTICHOKES sat in the corner. I ran my hand over the floor and felt nothing, not even a dust bunny. I checked again, searching for anything unpleasant: snakes, spiders, dead bugs, frogs . . . and found only my bedclothes, slightly rumpled, but empty.

I crawled into bed, tugging the covers up to my chin. I should have been happy to find my bed empty, but like the thought of dragons on the roof, it made me uneasy. Had Francesca gotten bored with the sand trick? Or had she thought of something worse? The first glimmer of moonlight trickled in the window; I eyed the lump that was Francesca. Maybe she'd gotten over her sister being dismissed; after all, it wasn't my fault. I decided I'd wait and see . . . and keep an eye out for anything wiggly or sticky or nasty that might take up residence in my bed.

As the moonlight poured across the floor, I studied each girl. That one was snoring. That one lay like a rock. That one tossed and turned. I gnawed on my knuckle, eager for them to settle into a deep sleep.

Butterflies wrestled in my stomach. I would need a good story to tell if I got caught wandering around in the middle of the night. I yawned. My covers felt warm and heavy. I snuggled in a little deeper.

Jane was in peril . . . one of the dragons stood over her, eyes glistening, fangs dripping, smoke writhing out of its nostrils. Jane held her hands out, warding off what she couldn't see.

"Give me your treasure," the dragon rumbled.

"I don't have anything," Jane sobbed.

"Nothing?" the dragon said, eyeing me hiding behind Jane. "What about her? She looks nice and juicy." The dragon raised a foot lined with sharp talons.

"Watch out!" I screamed.

I bolted upright in the dark, heart pounding, sweat trickling down my back. I kicked free of my tangled covers. For a moment, I'd thought the dragon had us, but I'd fallen asleep; it was only a nightmare. I peered around the pitch-black room. The moon had set. It was late; how late I couldn't tell. But I had to get going before dawn struck and the servants started rising.

I slipped out of bed. I would wake my mouse, run over to the west wing, grab Eighteen, and hightail it back here. And that would be that. No more adventures for me. I'd tell them that first thing tomorrow.

A furry feeling tickled the back of my hand. I jumped. A soft squeak sounded. I looked down. My mouse stood on my pillow, wringing his paws.

I knelt down on the floor so that I was eye level with him. "I'm sorry. I didn't see you. Are you all right?" I whispered.

The mouse nodded. Then he glanced anxiously at the floor.

"I didn't find any sand tonight," I told him. "But I saved you part of my bread and a slice of cheese."

He blinked and rubbed his tiny chin with his paw.

"Don't worry. It's okay if there isn't any sand to sweep. We can still be friends."

He drew himself up, placed his paw over his heart, and bowed low.

"Good. But tonight I need your help," I said.

He stood at attention, nose twitching.

"I left something in the west wing. Something important

that I have to get back. I left it in a room near the place where five mice . . . are . . . missing from the wainscoting?"

His ears twitched. His tail twitched. He rubbed one paw over the other.

"That's where you're from, isn't it?"

His tiny black eyes shifted from side to side.

"It's okay," I said quickly. "I won't tell anyone. We're friends, remember. I just need help finding that corridor."

He stood as still as the bedpost.

"Please," I said.

He shook himself all over. Then he nodded, almost to himself, and crept over to my hand. I turned it palm side up and he crawled in. He settled in my palm and put his paw to his forehead as if he were seeking something.

"You'll show me?"

He nodded. Then he streaked up my arm and nestled on my shoulder. I felt a tiny paw catch my hair. "Hold on," I said. He gripped my nightgown with his other paws, which tickled like a batch of beetles.

"I hope you can see in the dark," I whispered, feeling my way to the door.

Francesca kept the candles; I didn't dare use one to go walking through the castle. She'd be sure to notice if one burned down. I stumbled once, over someone's boot, biting my tongue to keep from squealing, but I made it to the door without waking anyone up. With a sigh of relief, I tiptoed out to rescue Eighteen.

I crept through the halls and wound down the stairs, keeping a sharp eye out for Guards. A curtain swayed in an archway waving tassels at me. Dark shapes loomed overhead. I kept low to the floor, darting from cover to cover. Chairs and sofas crouched at my side. I heard a faint call in the distance. I kept going. Fearless, accompanied by my faithful companion . . . I wrinkled my nose, skirting around another corner as I headed toward the west wing. I had no name for my mouse. I stopped short. Ahead lay the large oval landing above the main hall. I sank to my hands and knees.

Until now, I could have explained my wandering by some excuse like sleepwalking or a stomachache. But there was no excuse for leaving the east wing in the dead of night. I crawled over to the railing around the wide marble stairs leading to the main hall.

"Since we're friends now, I should introduce myself," I whispered to the mouse. "My name is Darling, and yours . . . ?"

He squeaked next to my ear, something that sounded a little like *eekahcho*. Not speaking Mouse, I wasn't certain I'd heard right.

"That's a good name," I said slowly, not wanting to hurt

his feelings. "But I'm not sure I can pronounce it. How about I call you Iago?" Iago was as close a name to the sound I'd heard as I could think of.

He patted my shoulder, which I took to mean that we had a deal. Just then heavy footsteps rang across the hall below me. I peered over the banister and saw Guards in pools of lantern light patrolling the gauzy twilight below. On the other side of the landing lay the entrance to the west wing.

"Almost there, Iago," I murmured, as much to myself as to him.

I held my breath, waiting until the sound of footsteps faded, and then crawled across the landing to the other side. Safe in the shadows, I stood up, rubbing my sweaty hands on my nightgown.

"Here's where I need help," I said. "I know I go down this corridor and turn left, and after that, I'm not sure where to go."

Iago released my hair, jumped off my shoulder, and rappelled down my nightgown like a mountain climber. He swung from my hem for a moment, and then dropped to the floor with a quiet *thump*. He twitched his tail, dropped to all four paws, and skittered off into the darkness.

"Hey!" I called in a loud whisper. "Not so fast."

He scampered on, unheeding. I ran after him, down halls and around corners, like someone had set a tiger after me. "Hey!" I called a little louder. He bounded down a stair without looking back.

I barreled after him. What if he got too far ahead of me? What if I lost him? I'd spend the rest of the night in a maze of corridors, never finding my way out until morning. I ran faster and slipped on a carpet, twisting my ankle and skinning my knee. A white streak blazed away from me in the dark.

After that, I limped along, hoping to catch sight of him. I would have to have a little chat with Iago if I ever came out of the west wing without getting caught. I stopped to catch my breath, leaning against a wall. I wiped my face and spotted him, hunched at the intersection of two corridors, trembling like a rabbit. I hobbled over to him, looking to see what frightened him. Ahead I saw a dim corridor lined with wainscoting. I walked over to it and brushed my fingers over it. Dancing mice. I turned around.

"Is this it?" I asked.

He squeaked back, but made no move to follow.

"Well? Are you coming?"

He rolled into a little ball of fur with two beady bright eyes pleading out at me.

"You're afraid of the corridor?"

He shook his head.

"Then what?"

His eyes darted toward the wainscoting.

"That?" I asked, pointing.

He shut his eyes and trembled. I waited, but it was clear he'd said all he had to say.

"Wait here," I said, and turned back to the corridor. Walls that had been peach were now a dingy gray lightened by the ghostly white of the wainscoting. I walked along, feeling for missing mice. Once I found them, I began to count doors. At the sixth, I stopped. As I put my hand on the doorknob, I took a deep breath. *Please. Please. If there's someone sleeping in here, don't let them wake up.*

The knob turned in my hand. The door swung open. I inched a toe across the threshold and onto the carpet. I strained to hear breathing. Silence. I slipped inside, easing the door shut behind me, only exhaling when I heard the quiet *snick* of the catch.

I'd made it. I was in the room. I glanced around. Pale light filtered through the crack in the curtains. It was almost dawn. I took in the shape of the bed and the wardrobe. I tiptoed toward the bed, but I couldn't see if anyone lay there in the shadows. I paused, swaying on my toes; it didn't matter if someone was in there. I had to get the dress, and get it now, before I lost my nerve. I swerved to the wardrobe, creeping along inch by inch. I froze as a floorboard creaked beneath me. Nothing happened. I continued my epic trek across the carpet. Had any explorer ever been so intrepid or so brave?

Had any Princess's Girl ever looked so silly tiptoe-ing around in the dark to fetch a magic dress? I grunted softly. No one would *ever* believe me about this. I found the wardrobe handle in the dark and pulled. The wood squawked in protest. A grumbling rose from the bed. My fingers turned to stone on the handle. My heart became a rock in my chest. The massive bed creaked and groaned as *someone* rolled over.

"Mercedes," a sleepy voice said.

I, Darling Dimple, Statue, stood unblinking and un-moving, mind blank except for the image of the rabbit-sized rats that would be my new friends in the dungeon.

The *someone* in the bed settled into a snore.

I blinked. My hand snaked into the wardrobe, slith-ering between linens, probing for the satiny feel of the dress. A fingertip grazed a cold spot in the pile. I knuckled my hand in deeper. Eighteen, silky, cold, and hidden, lay waiting for me. I grasped it and began tugging. It rolled into my hands, unfolding itself. I wadded it in my arms and turned to sneak away, not daring to risk closing the wardrobe door and causing another squawk.

The *someone* sat up in the bed. And yawned, stretching.

"Mercedes, fetch my tea," the voice whined.

There I was, Darling Dimple, Thief, red-handed with Queen Candace's dress in some stranger's bedroom as dawn broke through the curtains. My feet refused to help me by running. My tongue stuck to the roof of my mouth, unable to speak and talk me out of this. My brain refused to form an escape plan.

The *someone* flopped back on the bed. "Now, please," the voice slurred. And another snore erupted from the shadows.

I bolted then. I ran for it like that tiger really was after me. Across the room, out the door, down the corridor I raced. I didn't stop to see if Iago was waiting for me. I didn't stop to listen for Guards. I didn't stop for anything. My feet flew across the castle as if they could see a distant beacon that was invisible to me. And I didn't stop to argue with them.

I didn't stop until I was in the east wing, barreling up the stairs, clutching the trailing fabric of Eighteen, when I heard a sound that brought me to a halt. Afterward, it surprised me that I heard it because it was a small sound, an ordinary sound. It was the sound of someone whispering.

Whispering. You heard it all time, usually when you most wanted to hear what was being said but couldn't. This whispering was different, pointed and sharp. It cut through the quiet of the still-sleeping castle like one of Jane's knives.

"Don't let it go to your head," the whisperer said.

I sank against the wall of the stairwell and listened.

"She'll be like a purring kitten after this," a man's voice answered.

Who? Who would purr like a kitten? That was the problem with eavesdropping; you couldn't ask questions.

"Quiet," the whisperer hissed. It was a woman speaking, I could tell. "The walls have ears. If anyone overhears—"

I started, caught on the stairs like Princess Mariposa's *Lycaena alciphron* on a pin. If the whisperers came around the corner above, they'd see me. There was nowhere to hide. If I started back down the stairs they'd hear me. And catch me, Darling Dimple, sweaty, tired, and holding, oh, yes, that stolen dress—stolen from a dead Queen's closet, no less. I melted into the wall, hoping they'd go away.

"One butterfly does not seal a romance," the woman whispered.

Butterfly! I clamped a hand over my mouth to seal in the gasp waiting to explode out of it. They were talking about Princess Mariposa!

"She'll be mine before you know it," the man answered, sure of himself. "My charm is hard to resist."

I knew that voice; that was Prince Baltazar! He'd droned on all through the Ruby Luncheon.

"Indeed," the woman whispered drily. "Don't congratulate yourself yet. Stick to the plan."

"It's a beautiful plan," Prince Baltazar said. "A few butterflies for a kingdom."

Kingdom! He wanted Princess Mariposa's kingdom. He wanted her castle. He didn't love Princess Mariposa at all. I *knew* he wasn't fine enough for *my* Princess. My nails sank into my clenched palms; my blood boiled. She'd see through him! He'd never fool Princess Mariposa.

"Don't count your caterpillars before they hatch. Keep Mariposa too busy and too happy to think. Once a girl's head is turned, it's best to keep it turned."

"Not a problem, I assure you."

The woman went on as if she hadn't heard. "Once you are King, the regalia will be ours. And then we'll control the dragons."

"Yes, the dragons," Prince Baltazar hissed in an all-too-threatening tone.

My knees turned to water and I sank to the stairstep. These two meant to use the talisman from the King's regalia that controlled the dragons. And they were going to use the Princess to get it. Someone had to warn her!

Someone had to stop them.

I looked around, but there wasn't anyone there but me, Darling Dimple, Under-presser, squeezing Eighteen to her chest.

The ring of Prince Baltazar's boots sounded in the passage above—he was coming my way. I couldn't go up the stairs and it was too far down to escape before being seen. I had nowhere to go. I threw Eighteen over my head, melted into the white wall, and peeked out from under a flounce. Breath bated. Heart pounding. Fingers crossed. Wishing with all my might to turn invisible just then. Prince Baltazar appeared at the top of the stairs and walked on past, too absorbed in his evil scheme to notice a pile of creamy flounces trembling on the stairs.

Once his steps died away, I vaulted up the stairs. I'd find out who that woman was and then I'd do *something* to stop her! Throw Eighteen over her and trip her, maybe, or jump on her and scream for the Guards. Something.

At the top, I lunged around the corner. A flash of long dark cloak swirled around a distant arch as a tall, slim figure disappeared through it. *She was getting away!* I bounded after her, tripping over Eighteen and rolling into a wad of ruffles on the carpet. By the time I untangled myself, she was gone. Vanished. I looked up and down the corridor and around both corners, but there was no cloak in sight. I'd lost her.

How could I stop her if I didn't know who she was? In a castle full of people, she could be anybody.

15

By the time I got back, it was daylight. I raced to Queen Candace's closet, tossed Eighteen in, slammed the door, and bolted for the girls' dormitory. The sound of girls getting ready for the day filtered through the closed door. I dithered, shifting from one foot to the other. It was too late to sneak back to bed. They knew I was gone, but did they know how long I'd been gone? I yanked the door open.

Sunlight played around the room, dappling everything with the sweet kiss of morning. Girls pulled on stockings, brushed hair, and tied aprons. Nobody seemed to be looking for me. I yawned, a jaw-cracking, arm-flinging yawn, and sauntered in, scratching my side like a bear that'd hibernated through the winter. The sort of bear that couldn't possibly have been running around the castle with Queen Candace's dress or overhearing would-be criminals. The kind of bear that had gotten up only minutes before.

"It's time to get moving," Francesca said crisply.

I nodded as if she were right—I'd been too long in the bathroom—and ambled over to my bed to pull on my clothes. I wanted to fall across the bed in a swoon of relief—Francesca could accuse me of being slow just so long as she didn't guess the truth. I whipped on my clothes and picked up my brush.

I slid the brush in my hair and it stuck fast. I pulled again and my scalp screamed in pain. I heard a muffled twittering behind me. Tears started in my eyes. I felt something gooey drip down my forehead. I dabbed at it with a finger and a white glob coated my fingertip. *Glue.* Someone had poured glue into my hairbrush! That Francesca! No wonder my bedsheets had been sand-free. She'd dreamed up a new way to torment me.

I struggled with the brush, but the more I pulled, the more my dandelion-fluff hair twisted around it. A tear ran off the end of my nose. I stood, brush hanging in my hair, glue dripping down my scalp, back turned to the Princess's Girls, and fought the urge to bawl. The sand had been petty, but this was downright mean. I swallowed a lump of hot, unshed tears that burned down the back of my throat.

I squeezed my eyes shut. I would not turn around. I would not speak. I would not give them the satisfaction of seeing me miserable. I planted my feet like stone and set my face like iron. Gradually, the twittering ceased. And a long silence followed until I heard the last of them tiptoe guiltily out the door.

Only then did I let myself sob out loud, crying hot, angry tears until my nose ran and my eyes burned. And I was so late that Lindy would . . . oh, what did it matter what Lindy would do? I'd never get the brush free without yanking all my hair out. And I'd be a bald orphan with nowhere to go and no one to care and poor Princess Mariposa would marry that awful Prince—

The thought ricocheted through my mind, bringing me to my senses.

No matter what, I, Darling Dimple, would not stand for that! I would not let Prince Baltazar and the Cloaked Lady get their fingers on the talisman or hurt the Princess or release the dragons or wreck the castle. No. I. Would. Not.

I marched straight out of the girls' dormitory without any breakfast. The brush bounced painfully against my temple, as the roots of my hair cried out for relief, but I kept going, not stopping until I reached the pressing room.

"Don't that beat all," Lindy said. "That Laundress is blind as a bat! Grease stains!" She pointed to a ball gown of spring-green fabric draped over an ironing board.

"Are you sure that's not candle wax?" Cherice asked, squinting at the spots. "Candle wax we might scrape off, but grease! My dear, grease is another matter."

They both shuddered at the thought. They both lifted the cloth to their noses and sniffed.

"Grease," Cherice said.

"Grease, for sure," Lindy agreed. "I have a bottle of orange spirits in my cupboard—"

I coughed—loudly. They both looked up at the same time.

"Whatever did you do to yourself?" Lindy demanded.

Cherice dropped the folds of satin and took my chin in her hand. She turned my head this way and that, clicking her tongue. "Glue," she said.

"Glue?" Lindy exploded. "Darlin', what ails you? Whyever would you put *glue* in your hair?"

"I doubt she meant for it to find its way there," Cherice said.

"It wasn't me," I said, "it was—"

"An accident," Cherice finished, giving my chin a warning squeeze. "Lindy, my dear, spirits of orange! An excellent idea. Why don't you work on those spots and I will see what I can do with this?"

Without waiting for an answer, she spun me around and marched me across the room to the tub of water we used for pressing. Lindy, muttering about the worthlessness of Laundresses, opened her cupboard and began digging through its contents. Once we were out of earshot, Cherice shook my shoulder.

"Listen to me, my dear, tattling never cures the crime."

"But Francesca—"

"Shh. What proof do you have? See? None. And I promise you that whoever in this castle is punished for this, it won't be Francesca."

"It's not fair," I protested. But before I could say more, she plunged my head in the tub and began to work a bar of soap through my hair.

"No, it's not fair, my sweet, but believe me, it is the way it is," Cherice whispered at my ear. "Her mother will never allow her to be punished; some other girl will be dismissed as a consequence. Wouldn't you hate for that girl to lose her job because of you?"

I'd forgotten that the Head Housekeeper was Francesca's mother. Cherice was right; it wouldn't do me any good to complain. I shut up, wincing as Cherice dug my soapy hair out of the brush, bristle by bristle. I clenched my fingers around the tub's rim and grit my teeth. I had almost decided that I'd rather be bald when Cherice freed the last strand of hair. She tossed the ruined brush into a wastebasket and poured a pitcher of clear water over my head.

"There," she said. "Voilà." She handed me a towel with a flourish. "Cheer up, my dear, your hair is sparkling clean."

"Great," I said. I rubbed the towel into my sopping-wet hair while rivulets of water ran down my neck and soaked my collar. I'd find a way to deal with Miss Francesca myself. She wasn't going to get away with this.

Over at the ironing board, Lindy clutched a white cloth in one hand, a bottle of orange-tinted liquid in the other, and scowled. "Indolent, slack, good-for-nothing sluggard," she sputtered.

"I take it you have not had success?" Cherice said, winking at me.

"Success!" Lindy said, tossing the white cloth and the bottle on the ironing board. "Grease should be soaked out immediately, at once, if not sooner, not left to dry into this—this—this—" She gestured, too full of indignation to speak.

I glanced at the damp green satin and did not see any spots.

Cherice leaned over me. "Looks spotless to me," she said.

"There. There!" Lindy stabbed her finger at the cloth.

I squinted, looking hard at the spot where Lindy pointed. If there were stains, I couldn't see them.

Cherice squeezed my shoulder. Her cheek twitched in

amusement. "My dear, only those with the eyes of a hawk could see any spots! The satin is saved; all is well."

Lindy started to speak, but nothing more than a *harrumph* came out.

Cherice patted my wet head. "And our Darling, she still has hair."

Lindy glanced at me. "All that fluffy hair don't amount to much wet, does it?"

I shrugged.

Cherice laughed. "Someday Darling will grow up and have long flowing curls and be very pretty. And we will be old and jealous."

"Ha!" Lindy said, and picked up the bottle of spirits of orange.

I bit the inside of my cheek. I couldn't decide if Cherice was teasing or serious as she swept past me on her way out the door. Lindy set to work again on the spots only she could see. Behind her, I caught the sprawl of her possessions that had tumbled out of the open cupboard: a sunshade, a broom, a bucket, and a cloak.

A long black cloak. A cloak I'd seen her fling on and waltz away in day after day. Before now, I had never thought once about it.

A chill gripped me. Earlier that morning, I'd seen a long black cloak vanish around a corner. A long black cloak worn by the Cloaked Lady. Lindy the Head Presser was scheming with Prince Baltazar to find the king's talisman and release the dragons on the roof! If I hadn't seen it with my own eyes and heard it with my own ears—I'd never have believed it.

I realized right then that Francesca's tricks were the least of my problems.

16

Hours later, I had a crick in my neck from pressing and, at the same time, watching Lindy's every move. She flitted back and forth between her irons and her board, pressing a cascade of delicate laces with a series of different-sized irons. The smaller the flounce, the smaller the iron she used. Turn, twist, flex: each movement precise. I could picture her insides: gears, wheels, springs, ticking away like a clock. Acres of the finest fabrics flowed beneath her careful hands. Never scorch marks, never a blot, just smooth folds of cloth and lace, wrinkle-free and hanging on gilded hangers.

I had to admire that kind of efficiency.

It confused me. Who was Lindy really? Was she Lindy the Head Presser, devoted to eradicating wrinkles, or

Lindy the Cloaked Lady, whispering behind corners and plotting? I tried to picture that: Lindy, eyes wild, cloak blowing in the wind as she rode the back of a ferocious scaled monster. Could that be the real Lindy?

Deep down, I hoped it wasn't true. But maybe it was. The thought of the long black cloak inside her cupboard plagued me until my head spun.

I thought about Lindy's scalding tongue. It was a good thing the Head Laundress hadn't heard what she'd said about those spots. Down in the under-cellar, the Head Scrubber washed the priceless porcelain and crystal used by the Princess, the Scrubbers washed the regular dishes and silverware, and the Under-scrubbers washed the pots and pans—which, being metal, couldn't be broken. The Laundry worked the same way. Only the Head Laundress would be allowed to touch the Princess's gowns. Lindy had called her blind as a bat and a bunch of other things. The Head Laundress took pride in her work; she'd scald Lindy in one of her vats if she heard her say those things. Why wasn't Lindy worried about being overheard?

Then again, despite her temper, she hadn't swatted me like the Supreme Scrubstress had. Lindy got mad fast, but she got over it quickly too. It was hard to imagine her doing anything really terrible.

Lindy whipped open the cupboard door and my knees twitched. Out came her cloak. Out came that smile I'd seen a hundred times. "Finish up and get some lunch," she told me, and vanished out the door, whistling.

Who could eat at a time like this? I sprang after her. But I skidded to a stop at the door. What was I thinking? If she saw me follow her, she'd be suspicious. I mean, what excuse did I have? Lindy ate with the Head House-keeper and other important servants. I ate in the kitchens. I gnawed on my knuckle, deep in thought. How could I keep an eye on Lindy?

The dresses! I needed the dresses!

I raced to Queen Candace's closet, jerked open the door, and tripped over a pile of rags. I twisted my ankle for the second time in less than a day. Rubbing my sore foot, I looked to see what I'd fallen over.

Number Eighteen, lying where I'd tossed it last night. I scooped up the pile. Shreds of silk and remnants of ribbon slithered over my fingers, a tattered ruin. Every hint of magic was gone from the fabric as if it had never been there.

"Oh my goodness!" The dress that had yesterday been as new as the day Queen Candace had hung it on its silver hanger was rags. I gathered the remains of Eighteen in my arms and held them out to the canary.

"What happened?" I asked.

The canary eyed me sharply as if to say, *Don't you know?*

"No, I don't know," I said. I started for the hanger.

Maybe that's all it needed, hanger eighteen, and then it would be as good as new. The dresses bristled as I limped past. Nineteen flinched as though my touch were poison when I reached for the hanger. Gently, I laid the dress over it and hung it back up.

It hung, listing, a sleeve trailing by a thread, the skirt dragging the floor in spots. The air around me steamed with outrage. Eleven hung on its hanger, quiet and still, but still beautiful, still looking like new. It was asleep, but Eighteen was . . . dead.

"I'm s-sorry," I told the dresses. "Truly. I meant to bring it back, meant to hang it up, but . . ." I swallowed. I'd hidden it all day in the west wing and then left it on the floor for hours. The once-pristine Eighteen looked as if it had aged overnight. The sun glinted off the silver hanger's gold badge.

"That's it, isn't it?" I whispered. "You have to either be worn or on your hangers."

The canary flicked his tail and looked out the window.

"I didn't know," I said again. "I really didn't."

But deep down, I felt I should have. Eighteen had fought me when I'd tried to take it off. It had tried to tell me, but I hadn't listened. I was too afraid of getting caught.

A lump rose in my throat. I'd killed Eighteen and I couldn't undo it. I turned to go and the dresses shrank as if Darling the Dress-Murderer were going to snatch them off their hangers. I didn't blame them at all. I left, closing the door silently behind me.

Cherice was locking the door of closet number three. "The canary is well?"

"He's fine," I said.

"You mustn't let Francesca make you miserable," Cherice said. "Get some lunch—and put a ribbon in your hair! Young ladies should always wear ribbons."

I nodded, numb, and walked off on frozen feet with a frozen heart and a frozen mind. I had ruined one of Queen Candace's magical dresses. How could I ever make up for that?

17

Gillian beamed when she saw me. The Supreme Scrubstress let her workers eat early, before the dirty dishes started piling up, so I hardly ever saw her at lunch. I grinned back, glad she was there.

"So," I said, putting my plate down across from her. "What's up?"

"Roger 'n' me have a plan," she said.

I nodded, picking up my spoon. I hadn't had breakfast, so I dug right in.

"A plan to see the dragons on the roof," Gillian confided, stirring her soup.

"Wh-what?" I choked. "You are crazy." I glanced around to make sure no one was listening. "You can't go up to the roof; it's a mile above ground. You'd fall and break your neck."

"Jane did it." Gillian leaned closer. "She didn't fall."

"Well, that was Jane," I said. I tried to imagine Jane as a kid tiptoeing on a crossbeam, arms out, balancing a gazillion feet above ground. My head swam and my stomach gurgled in protest.

Gillian paused to blow on her spoonful of soup before adding, "The Supreme Scrubstress told me she was our age."

I swallowed hard. "Well, you don't know how to get up there, so that's that."

"Roger does," she said, waggling her eyebrows.

Dizziness washed over me as I remembered standing on the star on the Princess's terrace and seeing the dragon come into focus. I wasn't at all sure I wanted to see it up close.

"Scared?" Gillian whispered.

"I have work to do. I can't just go a-dragon-hunting for fun," I said, sounding a lot like Lindy. I winced.

Gillian grinned. "I think Roger likes you."

"No, he doesn't!" I shouted. Every head in the room turned. I felt my face burn. "No, he doesn't," I repeated in a steely, quiet voice. "We are just friends."

"Friends," Gillian said, dark eyes alight with a wicked gleam. "*Good* friends."

Heat crawled across my cheeks. I knew I looked like a poppy-red dandelion.

"I could ask him for you," she said, curling a dark lock around her finger.

"Do and I'll never tell you another story as long as I live," I said, pointing my spoon at her nose.

"You can't resist telling stories," she said with a laugh.

"You can't resist hearing them," I retorted.

"So," she said, eyes sparkling, "thought up any new stories lately?"

I wanted to tell her everything—all about Prince Baltazar and the dresses. But it all sounded like some story I'd made up; she'd never believe it. So I whiled away lunchtime telling her a story about a mouse who spied for a king. Not my best story, but good enough to satisfy Gillian for a day or two. At least until I could think up a better one.

Later when I arrived back at the wardrobe hall, Cherice stood in the door of closet number three, holding a fan out to Princess Mariposa.

"You should have sent for it." Cherice bit her lip. "If you are displeased with me—"

Princess Mariposa wore a gown embroidered all over with rosebuds and crystals. Her complexion turned as pink as the rosebuds. She snapped the fan open and waved it agitatedly.

"Oh, no. Of course not. It's warm today," Princess Mariposa said, flapping the fan faster.

"Did something happen at luncheon?" Cherice said.

At that, Princess Mariposa turned as poppy-red as I'd been in the kitchen.

"Don't be silly," Princess Mariposa said. "I wanted my fan."

Cherice looked unconvinced. It was a long walk from the luncheon tent, and there were dozens of servants who could have fetched anything the Princess desired. Before Cherice could comment any further, the Princess spotted me.

"My Darling Under-presser!" she exclaimed, and held out her hand.

I froze, eyeing the porcelain hand with its pearl-pink nails and gold rings. The Princess's own hand. Held out to *me*. She smiled encouragingly, wiggling her fingers. I took her hand.

"Have you seen my butterflies?" she asked.

"No, Your Highness," I said.

"Come with me," Princess Mariposa said, and walked off to her rooms.

"Your Highness! Luncheon. The princes—" Cherice called.

Princess Mariposa led me through a vast bedroom with the hugest bed I'd ever seen. It was so big that all the Princess's Girls could sleep in it at the same time. The bed curtains were purple velvet lined in blue satin. A coverlet of blue satin embroidered with purple-and-gold butter-flies sailed over the bed like a vast sea. A mountain of lace-trimmed pillows teetered against the headboard, which rose in great carved heights under the canopy. I wanted to see more, but the Princess tugged me along.

The next room flashed past in a wonder of green and silver, filled with tapestry chairs, inlaid mother-of-pearl tables, and golden candelabras with tall white candles. I saw a hint of books on shelves and smelled a whiff of lavender before we plunged into a long gallery. A gallery of ghost-white marble floors and white walls, white velvet curtains at white-trimmed windows. And a white ceiling high overhead that was covered in a million white butter-flies: each one hanging from the ceiling by a silver thread.

"Wh-whosh," I said. Which sounded pretty stupid, even to me, but all that white made me breathless.

And if *that* hadn't taken my breath away, the million *real* butterflies would have. Butterflies in cases, mounted in white picture frames, and set in white cabinets and cu-rios, added the only splashes of color to the room. If some-one had spilled a rainbow, that's what it would have looked like: a glimmer of green here, a gleam of orange there, a hint of purple, a speck of gold, a flash of blue. I turned around, drinking in the beauty of so many butterflies.

They were dead, of course, pinned by tiny steel pins to

cork or wood or velvet. A million, million fragile wings absolutely still. A trillion antennae hushed. Their tiny hearts quiet in their tiny chests. This made me scratch my head and wonder, *Do butterflies have hearts?* If they didn't, they ought to.

"Did you catch all of them?" I asked.

"Oh, no!" Princess Mariposa exclaimed. "No, only a few; most were gifts."

That made sense. I stepped closer to a cabinet and gazed through the glass. A large butterfly with a mosaic of yellow, black, and orange on its wings lay over a small silver plaque that read ZERYNTHIA RUMINA, GIFT OF HERMANN OF SYLVANNIA.

She leaned over me, tracing the glass top with a finger as if she wished she could touch them. "They come from all over the world. Some are common in their own countries, but some are very rare."

"Why do you collect them?"

She drummed her fingers on the glass. "Do you collect anything?"

I shook my head. A memory of the Supreme Scrubstress handing me the empty artichoke crate flashed through my mind. Would I ever own anything to put in it?

Princess Mariposa arched her eyebrow. "It seems silly, doesn't it? Keeping all this beauty hidden here? But . . . they remind me that true treasure can't be held in our hand, it can't be kept. It touches us, grazes our palm, and flits away. . . ." Her eyes darkened. "Once Eliora was known for its many beautiful butterflies, but they are gone now."

"Gone? Why?"

The Princess shrugged. "No one really knows. There are butterflies here and there, but not like there used to be. Perhaps something scared them away?"

"Dragons," I muttered under my breath. If I were a butterfly, I'd stay as far away from a castle with dragons chained to the roof as I could.

"Excuse me?"

"Um. How long have you been collecting them?" I asked, fumbling to cover my blunder. I wasn't supposed to know the secrets she'd told Teresa.

"Since I was ten."

"That's a long time," I said.

"Do you think so?" she said with a twinkle in her eye.

"Well . . ." I realized I had no idea how old the Princess was. And Jane had once scolded me for asking about *her* age. It probably wasn't the sort of thing you asked a Princess either. I bit my lower lip and twisted my hands together.

"Watch!" Princess Mariposa said.

She unlatched a window and threw it open. The afternoon breeze flowed in and the millions of white butterflies danced on the ends of their silver cords.

"Goodness!" My hands flew to my cheeks as I watched the whirlwind of butterflies above me.

The Princess laughed. "See! It always cheers me up."

"It cheers me up too!" I said.

And it did. But only for a moment, because the next moment I thought about Prince Baltazar's butterfly and his plot to snatch the kingdom from the Princess. But with all these competitors, the purple-shot copper didn't seem so exciting. Not nearly exciting enough to win the Princess's heart. I glanced around for that traitorous butterfly, but there were so many . . . a gold-lined casket on a cabinet top caught my attention. I gravitated toward it. An elegant white butterfly with black-veined wings lay inside next to a handwritten parchment. *To Princess Mariposa of Eliora, From Prince Humphrey of Tamzin,* in large loopy letters written at a slant as if some child had scrawled the message.

"Who's Humphrey?" I asked.

Princess Mariposa's smile melted. She toyed with her fan. "Humphrey was a boy I met when I was your age."

"Was he nice? His butterfly is pretty. It looks like stained glass."

"It's very pretty. He was a prince. A spoiled prince." A line creased her forehead.

"Was he a brat?" I asked. "I know some boys that are

brats." Like Roger, Mister Make-plans-with-Gillian-to-go-see-dragons. *My* Jane had seen them; he should have asked me to go first. Not that I wanted to.

"Yes, he was a brat. He called me Po Po!"

"That's terrible," I said. "What did you do? Lock in him a dungeon? Banish him to an island?" I could think up lots of great punishments for spoiled-brat princes!

"I called him Tubby." She spoke with a hard edge to her voice, gripping her fan.

I heard a faint *crunch* as the spines broke, and flinched.

"But he deserved it," she assured me. "He pulled on my curls. He put a spider in my soup. He didn't behave at all like a prince."

"Did you tell on him?"

She shook her head. "He was Father's guest."

"Did you ever see him again?" I asked, disappointed. I'd have told on him. *And stuck a spider in his soup.*

"No," she said. "Never again. But he sent me this butterfly."

I mulled that over. She met this spoiled prince who was mean to her and she never told on him and then he gave her this beautiful butterfly....

"You kept his butterfly," I said, stating a fact.

The Princess started as if this had never occurred to her before.

"I guess I did," she said, frowning. She glanced around as if somewhere lay the reason for her having kept it. She shook her head as if puzzled, tapping her fist with her fan.

"I guess I did," she repeated to herself.

I shifted from one foot to the other. It was awkward, standing there wondering what I'd said to make her act so strange. So I said, "Thank you, Your Highness, for showing me your butterflies."

"You're welcome," she said absently. "Run along now."

18

That night, I tossed and turned, my sleep haunted by dragons and butterflies. I woke in the darkness, panting from racing up and down nightmare castles. I needed someone to help me. But who? I'd tried after dinner to talk to Jane, but she refused to hear anything I said. She would not discuss dragons or princes or anything. She made a beeline for the Head Cook and struck up a conversation about puddings, of all things.

And if she wouldn't listen, no one else would. I'd told one too many stories for anyone to listen to me now. There was only me, Darling Dimple, Dragon-Thwarter, at hand to save the Princess.

Any Dragon-Thwarter worth their mettle will tell you that dragon-thwarting is not an easy business. A

Dragon-Slayer only kills dragons, usually with a big sword. A Dragon-Thwarter has to *thwart* the dragon without getting within claw's reach of him. Because Dragon-Thwarters like me lacked big swords, not to mention shields, armor, or those big heavy boots that Dragon-Slayers wear.

I planned to keep the entire castle's length between us. Just to be safe. I had to stop those dragons without grappling with them in person. The easiest way to do this was to tackle the problem of Lindy the Cloaked Lady and Prince Baltazar. And for that, I would have to follow them to find out more about their schemes.

I needed to make peace with the dresses. But I was a short on bright ideas as to how one made up with angry clothes. As I pondered this dilemma, something soft and warm curled up against my shoulder.

"Iago?" I whispered. "Is that you?" I felt my shoulder, touching the tip of his tiny tail. "It *is* you. Iago, I was worried."

He popped up on my chest and studied me. Nodding, he waved his tail around over his head, turned around twice, and shook himself.

"You were confused . . . you got lost twice? You were scared?" I guessed, still not very conversant in Mouse.

Iago bowed, curling his tail in a knot.

"And since then you've been tied up with . . . mouse business?"

He nodded sharply. I grimaced. What business did mice have to take care of? The four little mice, maybe? He saw my puzzled frown and put a paw to his brow as if looking for something. Then he pantomimed tiptoeing and looking.

"You've been looking for something?"

Iago dropped down on all fours and crept down my chest, darting behind a clump of bedcovers, and then popping up for a look before darting to another.

"Spying?" I breathed. "You've been spying?"

He tipped an imaginary hat to me.

"Who've you been spying on?"

Iago scampered up to my nose and stretched as tall as he could, his tail stiff behind him, his paws curled up like claws. He mimed breathing fire and slashing with his claws.

"Dragons?" I yelped, forgetting to whisper. The lump in Francesca's bed turned over. Iago froze. I held my breath and counted to a hundred. The lump settled back in. Exhaling, I whispered in as quiet a voice as possible, "You've been spying on the dragons? Why?"

Francesca mumbled in her sleep. Iago flicked his tail and vanished under the bed. I meant to demand that he explain what was going on, but just then someone else snorted in their sleep. I froze. I'd lie awake until everything was silent and then . . .

Something poked my shoulder. I opened my eyes. Francesca hung over me.

"Wake up!" She poked me again. "Darling, this is your last warning!"

I sat up, rubbing my eyes. "Warning for what?"

She snapped her fingers. "For tardiness! You've slept so long *all* the other girls are gone!"

I glanced around the empty room and bolted up. "Oh, gosh! Oh, no!" I scrambled around, yanking on stockings, dress, and apron. I shoved on my boots and hobbled to the door, grabbing at my trailing apron ties.

"No girl of *mine* goes out like this!" Francesca said, catching my apron and hauling me back. "Hold still." She tied my apron and slapped me on the head. "Brush this mop," she ordered, "and tie those boots!"

I plopped down to lace my boots. From the corner of my eye, I saw two black dots blink at me from under my bed. Iago. He'd been telling me something about dragons and I'd fallen asleep—

Francesca whacked me with a hairbrush. "Wake up!"

I shot up and balled my fist under her nose. "Don't ever hit me again!" I shouted. Her eyes widened; she fell back a step. Then her features hardened.

"Don't threaten me," she said. "One word from me and your little friend, what's her name . . ." Francesca put a finger to her chin and cocked her head. "Oh, yes, Gillian the Under-dryer, that's who. Will. Be. Gone. Understand?"

I understood that blood boiled in my veins. I understood that steam rose out of my ears. I understood that I could punch her to the ground and stomp on her.

"And that blind lady, Jane," Francesca continued, unaware that she was about to be pulverized. "She'll have to go too. We just can't have *her* sort around. She's a bad influence, raising a monster like you!"

At that, all the fight in me fizzled out like a match in a puddle. Where would Jane go if the Head Housekeeper tossed her out? How would she survive out there, stumbling along, unable to see? My shoulders slumped all the way down to my belly button.

"So you can see reason. Good. Brush your hair," Francesca said, holding out the brush.

I took it, checked the bristles for glue, and ran it through my hair. Then I tossed it back to her and turned on my heel. I walked away. An ember of resentment burned in my chest. She'd been mean to me from the start—all because of her stupid sister. I'd never even met her sister. And I didn't want to. She was probably just as rotten as Francesca. My fists curled; my steps quickened. If Francesca hadn't interfered, I'd have gotten to talk to Iago and probably learned something important, something a top-notch Dragon-Thwarter needed to know. The ember in my chest roasted away. The angrier I felt, the faster I walked. My heels were burning when I scooted into the pressing room.

My ironing board staggered under the pile of linens waiting for me. Lindy was gone, but a note was pinned to the pile.

Good work yesterday. Here are some new sheets. Give them special care.

Considering that the Princess had enough sheets to swaddle all the people in the kingdom with some left over for the horses, I couldn't imagine why she needed new ones. I wiped my hot, sticky palms on my apron. I didn't have time for this! I needed to find out what Lindy was up to. I had dragons to thwart. Plots to unmask. A prince to stop.

I needed a dress—now!

19

The canary eyed me like a yellow sentinel guarding a treasure from a barbarian horde. The dresses played dumb, hanging on their silver hangers all stiff and cool. They didn't fool me.

I planted a fist on my hip. "You know something is seriously wrong around here, don't you?" I told that canary. "There's a plot against the Princess."

Those black eyes stared back at me without blinking, but a feather in his tail twitched.

"A plot to release those dragons," I added.

The dresses stirred as if they were murmuring among themselves.

"I was careless with Eighteen. I didn't mean to hurt

anyone, but . . . well, I did. I am very sorry." I paused, letting that soak in.

Then I turned in a full circle so that they could see
how serious I was. A couple of dresses perked up, obviously interested. One dodged deeper behind the dress in
front of it. The rest waited, still stiff and cool.

"So, are you going to help me? Or are you going to stay
mad and let the castle be destroyed?"

The canary glanced at One Hundred. Closest to the
window, One Hundred basked in the warm morning light,
its satin shimmering like freshly fallen snow. I held my
breath; there was something special about One Hundred.
The whole closet held its breath too. Precious seconds
ticked by. Even now, Lindy might be on her way back,
might catch me leaving the closet.

Might start asking questions.

One Hundred shrugged its crystal-embroidered shoulders, throwing a rainbow of sparkles across the floor. My
breath escaped with a *whoosh*. The dresses relaxed. A black
sleeve poked timidly out from behind a sapphire taffeta. I
walked over to the sleeve. Number Forty-One: velvet black
as ebony with a high collar encrusted with pearls. Gold
swirls, leaves, and flourishes intertwined with more pearls
traced the dress's sleeves, bodice, and hem.

"You'll help?" I asked.

The dress extended its sleeve as if to shake hands. So

I shook it, careful not to crush the velvet. "Thank you," I whispered, and slid it off the hanger. The dress hit the floor. I hastened to scoop it up. It weighed as much as a loaded basket of laundry. Would I be able to walk in this?

There wasn't time to argue, so I stepped into the dress. For a moment, I tottered under the weight, but then the dress hugged me close and became as light as air. I looked in the mirror to see who I was now—a lady greeted me with laughing brown eyes and a sprinkling of freckles across her nose. She wore a navy-blue dress with a silver emblem pinned to the shoulder. A Lady's Maid.

"Perfect," I told the canary, peeking out the door to see if the coast was clear. "A Lady's Maid can go anywhere the Upper-servants go. I can follow Lindy almost anywhere."

The canary snapped his tail and shook out his wings.

"Thank you!" I called over my shoulder. Behind me the canary whistled sharply, but I kept going. I had a plot to foil and a dragon to thwart, not to mention a huge pile of sheets to press. I loped down the first available stairs. Where would Lindy be this time of the day? Could she be in the kitchens? In the laundry room scolding the Head Laundress? Outdoors? Lurking in a corridor? There were too many possibilities to count.

Was she slinking around in that black cloak? I paused midstride; I should have checked on that before I left. If she had the cloak on, then she'd likely be conspiring with

Prince Baltazar in a dark corner somewhere. I scratched my nose. Should I go back and see if the cloak was gone? What if she was at her ironing board? What excuse could I make for being there? I didn't even know who I was supposed to be or whose servant this was . . . all the Princess's Ladies wore gray or silver, but this lady wore navy blue. This meant that she was someone else's servant.

I drummed my fingers on the banister. I'd take a look around the first floor. I'd act busy; Lady's Maids usually looked like they were very busy. What exactly they were busy doing, I couldn't imagine. But they always looked very busy doing it.

When I reached the first floor, I turned sharply toward the west wing and strolled past the throne room, head high, brow furrowed. The doors to the throne room were open, revealing a bustling scene inside. Princess Mariposa stood at the foot of the throne, flanked by Prince Baltazar and Prince Sterling, gazing up at a Footman who juggled a massive portrait up a ladder behind the throne. A throng of onlookers oohed and aahed. I stopped to gape at the portrait.

It was of a dark-haired man in a crown ringed with emeralds. Gold and pearls bespeckled his robes and a huge ruby gleamed on his chest. One hand held a scepter topped by a diamond the size of my fist. The other held a gold-clasped book. His fingers glittered with rings, and a gold cuff graced each wrist. But the thing that arrested my steps was the expression in his deep blue eyes. He looked right at me! Me, Darling Dimple, Imposter. His gaze drew me into the throne room. I stood gawking at him as people jostled around me.

A plump hand accosted my elbow. "Dorothia, whatever has taken you so long? Where's my shawl?"

I snapped out of my reverie. "Shawl?" I said.

The well-cushioned lady beside me shook my arm. "Did you not find it?" The woman looked like a popped-over soufflé in a lemon-colored gown with a high-piled swirl of white hair. Every inch of her glittered, from the pile of chains on her bosom to the stack of bracelets on her arm. Rings pinched her thick fingers and bobbed at her sagging earlobes.

The lady squeezed my arm impatiently. "Dorothia! Really, you must attend to what I say. My paisley shawl, the one dear Cousin Alfonso sent." The woman's eyes narrowed; she glanced down at my elbow between her fingers.

I froze. I might look like Dorothia, but I had the knobby elbows of a slightly-tall-for-her-age eleven-year-old. She dropped my arm, lips pursed.

"I'll be speaking to Pepperwhistle about this," she said. "She assured me that you were reliable."

Mrs. Pepperwhistle, the Head Housekeeper. If there was one person I did not want to see, it was her. I began to apologize, but the lady turned away.

"I mustn't miss anything. Run, fetch that shawl," she growled.

At that moment, a ripple went through the crowd and everyone rushed forward. The lady disappeared from view. A knot of servants hovered at the side of the room. I wormed my way over there, hoping to disappear among them. A drumroll sounded. The crowd fell silent. I rose on tiptoe to see over the shoulder of the man ahead of me.

"Good people, the portrait of King Richard once again graces our castle!" Princess Mariposa announced. "Our royal Artists have restored this masterpiece beyond our greatest expectations."

Applause broke out. I clapped harder than the rest. King Richard, the dragon-tamer! And he'd been painted with his regalia—I nearly gasped out loud. Somewhere in that picture was the talisman that bound the dragons! I squinted, swaying on my tiptoes, trying to see the details, but I was too far away.

Prince Sterling whipped a handkerchief out of his coat and offered it to Princess Mariposa. Smiling up at him, she dabbed her beautiful blue eyes. A shaft of sunlight fell on the two of them as they stood at the foot of the throne. The sun highlighted the worn spots in his brocade coat, but it also lit his brown hair and put a sparkle in his brown eyes. He might not be as muscled as Prince

Baltazar, but he radiated goodness as he patted Princess Mariposa's arm.

"He'd have been proud of you, Your Highness," Prince Sterling told her.

She flashed her most dazzling smile. "You think so?"

"I do," he replied. The servants around me murmured their approval.

"Well, my dear," Prince Baltazar said, sweeping Prince Sterling aside, "I have waited for just the right moment to present you with this gift. And what more auspicious occasion could there be? His Highness is back in his place, Your Highness is putting the sun to shame with your glory, and I am holding your heart's desire in my hand."

He extended a small cloth pouch to the Princess, who took it with a puzzled smile.

"My heart's desire?" she said. "How could you know my heart's desire?"

He couldn't know it! I balled my fists.

"Open it," he said with a flash of his big white teeth.

Princess Mariposa loosed the silk cord that bound the pouch and peeked inside. Her puzzled smile dimmed. "Seeds?"

"Not just seeds, my dear. These seeds are from the most prized plant in my kingdom, a *Buddleja*."

"Thank you," the Princess said, closing the pouch.

Prince Baltazar took it from her and spilled its contents into his palm. "The butterfly bush," he said.

"Butterfly bush?" The Princess stepped closer and peered at the tiny seeds.

"Shrubs that are a siren call to butterflies," Prince Baltazar crooned. "Its blooming stalks produce a nectar irresistible to *all* butterflies. Your kingdom, my dear, will once again be filled with the flutter of their multicolored wings."

An awestruck wonder flooded Princess Mariposa's face. My thoughts darted to her butterfly room and her sorrow over her kingdom's shortage. *This* was what he'd meant when he'd said, *A few butterflies for a kingdom.* I wanted to scream at her not to listen to him.

"A small token of my deep love for Your Majesty," Prince Baltazar said in a voice trembling with false feeling.

"Oh," she said. The wonder in her blue eyes—that rightfully belonged to the seeds—colored that scheming prince with a luster he didn't deserve.

Princess Mariposa laid her hand on his. "You have seen my heart's desire," she murmured just loud enough to be heard, "when no one else has."

I knew right then that it was over. Prince Baltazar and Lindy had won. They'd fooled her. She'd marry him, and any day now they'd have the regalia too.

I could almost hear the dragons on the roof thrum with pleasure.

20

After that, everyone jollied through their work, whistling, certain that *finally* their Princess had met her prince. Everyone but me. Discouragement weighed on me as I ironed away under the lashing gaze of the triumphant Lindy.

"There," she said, "didn't I always say she'd find someone? Didn't I?"

"My dear, you always did!" Cherice cooed.

I didn't remember her saying any such thing, but when Lindy poked me in the ribs and asked, "Didn't I, Darlin'?" I nodded, a fake grin plastered on my face. The last thing I needed now was for Lindy to suspect me of knowing anything. The Princess needed me; I was the only one in the castle with enough sense to see what was really going on.

But when Lindy and Cherice left for tea, I stood scowling at my iron.

"Fancy place you have here," I heard Roger say with a whistle.

Startled, I jerked around. Gillian and Roger stood beside me. Her sleeves were wet to the elbow and wet spots dotted her skirt. His face had a fresh-scrubbed pinkness, but his cap still bore its ostrich-in-a-hair-bow stain.

"What are you doing here?" I asked.

"We have it!" Gillian announced, pushing Roger aside.

I frowned. "Have what?"

"The key," Roger said.

"To the roof!" Gillian crowed.

I set the iron down on the stove and closed the vent to dampen the fire.

"We are going dragon-hunting." A fat iron key *whizzed* as Roger spun it on his finger.

They had the key.

"I never thought you'd get it," I said.

"Told you so," Gillian said.

A sudden coldness sent a shiver down my back. Dragon-Thwarters did not climb out on dragon-infested roofs. Not ones with any sense anyway. And certainly not with an overeager Under-dryer and a Second Stable Boy, neither of whom had any clue how to ward off horseflies, let alone dragons. I cast around the room for a good excuse to stay where I was.

I snapped my fingers. "Spirits of orange."

The two glanced at each other.

"I have something that will clean your cap," I said, and hurried over to Lindy's cupboard. "It's called spirits of orange and Lindy uses it on the Princess's dresses. It's right here." I scrabbled through Lindy's things, brushing her black cloak aside, and hearing a rustle in its side. I paused and ran my hand into the cloak. A paper crackled in a hidden pocket. I pulled it out.

Meet me tonight at the base of the western tower.—B.

I swallowed. She was meeting Baltazar tonight. Tonight!

"We haven't got all day," Roger said. "Either you're coming or—"

"Right here," I said, producing the bottle with one hand and stuffing the note in my apron with the other. "Give me your cap."

Roger slid his cap off, making a face at Gillian. I ignored them and set to work sponging the stain. The two leaned over my shoulder, eyes glued to the cap as the stain faded away. "There. Good as new." I handed Roger his damp cap. "It'll dry in a second."

"Huh." Roger's freckled brow puckered. "It's gone." He smiled broadly as he planted his cap back on his sandy hair. "Thanks."

Gillian rolled her eyes. "Stop stallin'."

"I'm not stalling," I said, tidying up my pile of towels, hoping that Lindy would waltz in and stop us. But she didn't. She never popped up when you wanted her.

"Are you coming," Gillian said, throwing her hands up, "or are you too scared?"

"Darling's not chicken," Roger said.

He didn't think I was chicken. I *had* to go now. I could stand it if he thought I was a daydreamer, but a chicken? No.

"I can't wait to see those dragons," I lied, rubbing my hands together as if ready for a dragon-sized fight.

Roger led the way and Gillian bounced after him. I followed just fast enough that they couldn't accuse me of dragging my feet. I kept looking over my shoulder, hoping someone—anyone—would catch us and send us back.

As we climbed higher into the north wing, I hoped that they only *thought* they knew where the door was. Maybe we'd never find it, or maybe they had the wrong key, or maybe the key was so old it would break in the lock. That last thought was particularly consoling; I'd look brave for going, but nobody could open the door—*ever*.

In the highest tower, we found ourselves on a narrow staircase twisting upward into a darkness pierced here or there by a window slit in the tower wall. Cobwebs stirred in the wake of our passing. We mounted each step with care as if they were slippery. Debris rustled underfoot. I held my apron close to my legs, anxious not to soil my clothes. I'd have a hard time explaining to Lindy how I got dust and grime on myself while pressing snow-white towels.

A great iron-bound door guarded the top of the stairs like a hulking ogre. The keyhole glared at us like a single black eye.

"One hundred and sixty-three," Roger said, puffing as he reached the top step.

"Whew," Gillian added, wiping her brow dramatically and nearly elbowing me in the eye.

"Looks heavy," I said. "We might not be able to open it."

"Jane and Marci did," Roger said with a shrug, and fit the key into the lock. It turned as though greased. The door swung open like a dancer on her toes. So much for the look of the thing, all that wood and iron.

Outside, I blinked in the bright sunlight. The crossbeam was the high point of the northern wing, with the roof sliding off from it in either direction. A narrow strip a few inches wide topped the beam, crossing the wing to the silver-capped white spire in the center of the castle. Vague gray shapes hunkered at the spire's base.

Roger whistled.

"Looks like a mile across," Gillian said, her curls tossing in the wind. She turned to me, a pink spot glowing on each cheek. "You first!"

"Me? Why me first?"

"Why not you first?"

"This was your idea."

"Was not."

"Was so."

"Afraid?" she said.

I planted both hands on my hips. "Maybe you don't want to go first because *you're* afraid?"

"Am not," she said, sounding unsure.

"Oh?" I said archly. "I dare you."

A sudden gust of wind tugged on my apron and pulled Roger's cap off his head, sending it flying to the center of the crossbeam. "Hey," Roger hollered, and stepped out onto the crossbeam. Immediately, he began flailing his arms and twisting for balance. I reached out and snatched the waistband of his pants and pulled back. My polished boots slid on the smooth beam. Gillian grabbed my waist and we fell back onto her in a pile.

"Oof!" she groaned. "Get off, get off."

Roger and I rolled off her and back into the shelter of the doorway. The green cap trembled in the breeze where it lay.

"My boots are too wide," Roger said, eyeing the crossbeam. "It was finally clean, too," he mourned, referring to his cap.

I stared at his boots and mine and Gillian's. Gillian was slim, but she had duck feet. Mine were narrow. If anyone was going to rescue the cap, it would have to be me.

"Only as far as the cap," I muttered to myself.

I stepped onto the beam, one foot in front of the other. One step at a time. Sweat broke out along my hairline. The wind flared up and tugged on me. The cap hopped once or twice in the wind, but stayed where it was. If it flew off the beam, that was it. There would be no reaching it; the tiled sides were too steep to step down on. I stood still until the wind died. I chewed my lower lip and glanced down.

A wave of nausea broke over me as the emerald lawn thousands of miles below swam up at me. I squeezed my eyes shut.

"Don't look down," Gillian called.

"Use your arms!" Roger yelled.

Sweat dripped down my nose. I took a deep breath, held my arms out straight from my sides, and walked. Just as I reached the cap, a blast carried it up and over, sending it to land on one of the gray humps. There it waffled in the wind, stuck tight, caught on an outcropping . . . a horn, maybe? I swallowed.

Did dragons have horns? Was that really a dragon? It looked very dragonish, all curving and spiny and long. *It's turned to stone. It's held by the collars. It's just a big rock. Nothing but a rock.*

A rock that grew bigger as I approached, until it loomed up from the base of the spire. Lines traced through the gray stone—scales, the spines of its wings, and the curve of its claws. The cap fluttered on one of its horns, shadowing its stone eyes.

I stepped onto the base of the spire, grateful to lean against its solid surface and catch my breath. A cloud passed overhead, darkening the hollows of the stone dragon. The faint beating of a heart appeared in the stone chest, and under the stone eyelids, a shadowy eye moved as if in a dream.

Whatever dragons dreamed about could not be good.

"Can you get it?" Gillian yelled.

"Come back. It's just a cap," Roger called.

Gathering my courage, I reassured myself that it could not wake up. I slid over to it and stretched out my hand. I stretched up as far as I could, but my fingers fell on empty air. I jumped and grabbed for it, scraping my knee on the dragon's rough stone hide. The cap was too far away.

To reach it I'd have to climb up the dragon; I thought I was going to be sick. Just then a tiny white mouse popped up from behind the cap and saluted me.

"Iago," I breathed in relief. "Can you get it?"

Iago took the brim in his mouth and worked the cap free from the horn. Then he opened his mouth and let it fall to me. I caught it and clutched it to my chest, dizzy with relief. Iago scurried down the dragon and dived for my shoulder, landing with a quick pinch of his tiny claws.

"Thank you."

"*Echaeek,*" he whispered in my ear urgently.

"I don't understand," I said, and held up a hand for him.

He climbed down into my hand. With a puckered brow, he pointed to the eye of the dragon and then to me.

"It's watching me?" I guessed, faint at the thought.

Iago nodded solemnly. He held out his paws, pretending to hold out a skirt.

"Because of the dresses?" I whispered, dry-mouthed. "Is that what you wanted to tell me the other night?"

He nodded, tail twitching. Then, quick as a flash, he dived back behind the dragon.

I held the cap and stared up at the dragon. Under that

icing of stone, it was watching. I felt it. The cloud overhead sailed off and sunlight hit the stone, glimmering gold in the thick folds of the dragon's neck.

The collar. I could see it plainly now, though I hadn't before. It was broad like the sort used on mastiffs, with spikes protruding from it and swirling letters inscribed in it. SARVINDER, it read.

Roger and Gillian whistled behind me, stomping their feet and clapping.

I turned away from the dragon, squinting. They looked small against the acre of roof. They hadn't seen Iago from where they stood. Or the collar. Or the dragon's eye moving. They had no idea what we were all up against.

What had Jane seen when she and Marci came up here? Had it scared her as much as I was scared now?

21

You'd have thought Roger and Gillian had touched noses with the dragon, the way they swaggered back down the stairs. I led the way, taking them two at a time.

"I wasn't scared," Gillian said, her voice echoing off the stone walls, "not even a little bit. If it hadn't been so windy—"

"Did you see the wind blow my cap right to Darling?" Roger let out a low whistle. "Good catch," he said. "Now that we have the key—"

I slammed to a stop. "Where did you get that key?"

"The Head Steward's office." He grinned so hard that another freckle popped out.

"We have friends in low places," Gillian said.

That meant it was an Under-servant who had access to

the Head Steward's office. I snapped my fingers. "A Messenger Boy!" They grinned like idiots. I fought down a frown. Stupid Messenger Boy—he could get fired for taking a key.

"You have to give it back before someone gets in trouble," I told them.

"Nobody will miss it; nobody ever goes up there," Gillian said. "I got a great hiding place down below."

"Oh, no, I'm keeping it." Roger wagged the key under Gillian's nose. She stepped on his foot. He shoved her in the shoulder. So she swatted his cap down over his eyes.

"Hey!" he hollered, pushing his cap up.

He swung at her and lost his grip on the key. It hit the stone step with a *clang* and bounced down a step to me.

The key melted into the shadow of the step like a crouching rat. It was just an iron object, but it was dangerous in the wrong hands. I pictured Prince Baltazar with that key clenched in his fist, bolting up these steps, unlocking that door . . . loosing that dragon.

I snatched it up. "It'll be safe with me."

"No!" they yelled. But the key was already in my pocket.

Roger jumped down to my step. "I got that key. How come you get to keep it?"

"Because," I said, flushing as he leaned in nose to nose.

"Because why?" His freckles were even sandier up close.

I couldn't think of a single good reason; all I could

think was that if I had it, Baltazar wouldn't get it. "Because I'm an Upper-servant." The words popped out.

Roger turned so red his freckles disappeared. Gillian froze, mouth open, curls swaying. For a moment, they both looked so hurt that I'd have done anything to take it back. Then they pushed past me, walking down the steps without a backward glance.

"Wait!" I cried. "I didn't mean that. I only meant . . ." I trailed off as they disappeared around a turn in the tower.

I trudged down the steps and went back to pressing towels.

As the afternoon faded, Lindy grew more animated. Her cheeks glowed. Her eyes sparkled. She stopped at the mirror to brush her hair to a glossy sheen. Then she popped a tiny pot out of her apron pocket and outlined her lips with a rosy ointment. She waltzed over to the cupboard. I swallowed hard; I knew what was coming—the long black cloak, the meeting with Baltazar, and my chance to stop them.

Lindy swirled into the cloak and danced out the pressing room door. I counted to ten. I had to grab a dress and be after her—close, but not too close. I didn't want her spotting me—er, *whoever* I'd be.

The canary greeted me with a sprightly melody. The dresses rustled on their hangers.

I hesitated. When, exactly, did *Meet me tonight* mean?

Seven o'clock? A quarter to nine? What if Baltazar didn't show up until midnight? I could be out until the doors were locked. I could be locked out until morning. Then I'd have to walk back up to the closet without running into someone who recognized the *whoever* I was supposed to be but wasn't.

It would be so much easier if I had someone helping me. A lookout who could run for the Guards if I needed them or unlock the door and let me back in. Someone I could trust.

Someone like Roger and Gillian. Neither of whom was ever going to speak to me again.

I sighed. Dragon-thwarting was a lonely business.

The hangers tinkled; the dresses were growing impatient.

"I have to go outside, and I need one of you to go with me," I told them. "I don't know how long I'll be gone, but I promise *not* to take you off until I return you to your hanger."

A skirt dipped out of the line of dresses on my right. Number Sixty-Four: moss-green velvet trimmed in bands of chocolate brown. The dress had a fitted bodice, full puffed sleeves, and a wide skirt. I slipped into it. It wrapped me in a velvet grip. The lady in the mirror wore a cranberry-red dress, the sort ladies wore to dinner. I smiled at her and she smiled back. Her smile had a mischievous glint.

"Are you ready for dinner?" I asked.

Her brown eyes twinkled. She was ready.

The first shadows of evening fell as I reached the juncture between the north and west wings. I had a plan: I'd slip unseen down the west staircase while everyone else was at dinner and hide near the tower's base. When Lindy appeared, I'd see her.

It was a foolproof plan.

Except that a slight figure stood at the top of the west stairs: a woman wearing a silver chatelaine weighed down with keys. Ebony braids were coiled at the nape of her neck. She turned, her gray eyes taking my measure in an instant.

"Lady Rachel," she said, her voice mellow like an oboe. "May I offer you my assistance?" She fingered the brooch at her collar—a silver butterfly set with marcasite.

I gulped. Mrs. Pepperwhistle, the Head Housekeeper. Sixty-Four gripped my waist protectively.

"Are you unwell?" Mrs. Pepperwhistle stepped closer. "Shall I summon a physician?"

I shook my head, stupid with terror. Her eyes quizzed me up and down. Any minute now, she'd touch me. She would know that I was not who I appeared to be.

"Very well," she said. "I don't mean to detain you, but I can't advise you to use this staircase." She glided to the banister.

I stumbled after her. Hammering rang from the floor below. I leaned over the banister and caught a glimpse of workmen.

"I am having this stair repaired. By the time the Princess has finished dining, it will be like new. All this will be cleared away," she said, standing at my elbow, "as if it had never been." *As if it had never been;* her low voice sent a shiver down my spine.

I lurched backward, sputtering, "Th-thank you, Mrs. P-Pepperwhistle. I—I'll use another stair."

I felt her eyes boring into my back as I hurried toward the main staircase in the south wing. I rounded the turn, barely able to restrain myself from collapsing against the wall in relief.

I'd make a quick trip down the south stairs and double back to the west wing. Down the corridor, a knot of people lingered on the main landing. A flash of cranberry red caught my eye. Lady Rachel hovered at the edge, toying with her fan and talking to a rapt gentleman.

Sixty-Four squeezed me, twisting sideways. I halted in midstride, casting about for a good place to hide. A thick pillar greeted me to my left. I ducked behind it and peeped around.

A bell sounded. The knot of people dissolved and flowed down the stairs. I saw the sweep of Lady Rachel's cranberry-red dress as she melted into the crowd.

"That was close," I told Sixty-Four.

A man in a shabby coat stayed several steps behind. Prince Sterling. I grinned, wondering how many courses were on the evening's menu card. He glanced around at the emptying landing, then paused and nodded at a shadowy corner before going on.

What was he nodding at?

I watched that corner as the shadows darkened and the outline of a man became apparent. He was tall and muscular; he wore gray like most servants, but his bearing was more like the palace Guards than the Footmen. His eye fell on me and I almost gasped out loud.

A minute ticked by before he vanished down the opposite corridor. I crept out from behind the pillar and made my way shakily down the stairs. The echo of the throng ahead told me which direction they'd gone.

To my right, double doors opened as if by magic—though really servants opened them—and Prince Baltazar escorted Princess Mariposa into the hall. She shimmered in a gown of grayish-lavender sparkling with amethysts. The jewels hugged her slender wrists and wove through her ebony hair. A flash of lightning from the windows illuminated the hall, leaping from jewel to jewel and outlining every one of her curls. I caught my breath; she gleamed like a star stepped down from the night sky.

"Oooh," I breathed.

Rain pattered against the glass panes. Sixty-Four twisted sharply about my knees. The Prince and Princess moved on down the hall. I watched them go. If I let them walk ahead of me, I could slip into the west wing without being seen.

Another flash of lightning sent Sixty-Four into a spasm. It wound so tightly around my knees, I nearly toppled over.

"Behave," I whispered, and yanked hard on the skirt.

A *rrrrip* sounded down the hall. The Prince and Princess turned. A hole gaped at me from the torn waist of the moss-green velvet. I gulped.

"Hello?" she called.

I stood stock-still. I'd been lucky when Teresa had been too shy to appear at the Ruby Luncheon, but Lady Rachel had already gone to dinner. She sat there that very moment.

"It was the storm," Prince Baltazar said with a laugh. "Nothing alarming."

"I am not alarmed," the Princess said, turning to leave. "My only enemies are boredom and caprice. It's a common fault in young men. Ardent one day, cool the next. The woods are positively full of fickle young men."

"But I, Your Majesty, am granite," Prince Baltazar replied.

Don't trust him! I wanted to yell, but the shadows swallowed them. Granite. Baltazar was more like oil, oozing and slippery, running where it wasn't wanted.

I headed after them, keeping close to the shadows, leaping past the lightning-brightened windows. The iron key in my apron pocket banged against my leg.

I heard the laughter from the dining room before I saw the light spilling into the dark hall. I ducked behind a drapery as the Princess waited for the Footman to announce her arrival. Another flash of lightning doused my dress.

Number Sixty-Four hunched against my waist. The tear gaped like a raw wound. Sewing wasn't one of my skills. Perhaps Cherice would help me repair the dress. I'd think up some story about how I'd noticed the damage. Later.

The dining room doors *clang*ed shut. I relaxed a little and imagined myself as Lady Rachel, spy for Her Highness, infiltrating a rival castle. Rain lashed the windows and lightning flickered down the halls. Sixty-Four winched its way up my legs. The farther I went, the fiercer the storm grew. Sixty-Four wriggled its way up my thighs and spooled around my waist. An expanse of white apron and silver-gray skirt showed beneath the moss-green velvet.

"Stop it," I told the dress. "Are you trying to get us caught?" I unrolled the fabric back down over my clothes.

The west wing looked different in the bluish glaze of the storm. Angles seemed off. Corridors appeared longer. It took me some time to find the hall that opened out to the base of the western tower and by then, rain pelted the castle, driven by howling wind. It was not a nice night to stroll outside.

Sixty-Four agreed; its sleeves puckered up my arms and its skirt coiled around my hips. I squinted through the pane at the side of the west door, but the rain kept me from seeing anything.

"I'll make a dash for it," I said, and put my hand on the door latch. I'd be soaked to the skin in minutes.

Sixty-Four reared up and bucked.

"I told you I needed to go outside. You volunteered," I reminded it.

Sixty-Four shuddered like a Duster who has broken a vase and been sent to the Head Housekeeper for dismissal. The shudder vibrated through the fabric and all the way down to the pit of my stomach. My fingers slid off the latch.

"What's wrong?" I whispered.

A fresh volley of rain hit the windows. I heard a creaking outside as if something had blown loose. I reached for the latch; Sixty-Four crackled as I moved, as hard as a lead dress. I stopped, hand in midair.

"Eighteen went outside with me and that didn't hurt it any."

I had hurt it by leaving it off its hanger in a pile, though. Eighteen was nothing but rags now. I hadn't listened when it had tried to warn me. Lightning blazed against the rain-streaked glass. Sixty-Four shuddered again.

"You can't get wet," I said, stepping back. "Or you'll . . . you'll die," I whispered, the words bitter on my tongue. "I won't let that happen; I won't go out."

Sixty-Four sagged around my ankles with a tangible relief. The note burned a hole in my pocket; I was so close. Lindy was out there meeting Prince Baltazar and I was stuck inside. I couldn't give up and go back. I might not have another chance like this one.

Recessed windows with thick curtains guarded each side of the main west door. I hurried over to one and flung the drapery aside. A shallow bench sat concealed in the window box. I curled up on it and pulled the curtains over me. I would wait there with an eye on the window for Lindy's return . . . or for the rain to stop, whichever happened first.

Sixty-Four settled around me with a celebratory air. I petted its soft velvet sleeve. "There, there, you're safe," I crooned. The windowpane felt cold against my cheek; the rest of me toasted in the heavy clothes. My stomach growled. I hadn't had my dinner. Dragon-thwarting was proving to be a hungry occupation.

The rain died down. The shadows darkened in the hall. I starved as the hours dragged by. My head nodded a few times, snapping up when I finally heard the door rasp open and a light, quick step on the marble floor. I peered around the drape; a dark-cloaked figure hurried off into the darkness. I hurried after her.

A voice carried down the hall. "Good night, Your Majesty," it said. *Prince Baltazar.* How did he get back here without my seeing him? Come to think of it, no one had gone out that door all evening. I'd have heard. Had he met Lindy? How was that possible?

I stifled a yawn and hurried back upstairs. By the time I reached Queen Candace's closet, Lindy was nowhere to be seen. I hung the dress on its hanger and went over to the window to fish the note out of my pocket. Moonlight flooded the room. *Meet me tonight . . .* She'd been there. Had he?

The canary fluttered in his cage. I folded the note and tucked it under the birdcage. I'd missed my supper for nothing.

"Hold on to that for me," I told the bird.

He flicked his tail at me. The moonlight bleached his feathers to a ghostly white. His black beady eyes sparkled. *Much prettier flying free,* I remembered Prince Sterling saying about Prince Baltazar's butterfly.

"I bet you get tired of being cooped up in there."

He bounced on his claws, shaking out his neck feathers. It was late, nobody was around, and a quick taste of freedom wouldn't hurt him. I flicked open the little gold clasp. He hunched on his perch like a ball of fluff. The

180

little wire door *twang*ed open at my touch. The dresses stirred on the rods. I slid my hand in the cage and the canary took hold of my finger. I brought him out. A tuft of feathers on his head blew up, fluffed by my breath.

"Just a quick trip around the room and then you have to go back."

The canary quivered on my finger and then shot straight up in the air. The hangers clanked together as the dresses' empty sleeves strained to reach him. He circled overhead, flapping frantically.

"Are you all right?" I asked. I'd never seen him behave so strangely, like a kite straining against a string.

With a scream, he flung himself down and straight at the stained-glass canary in the window. I heard a *pop*, followed by a brilliant flash of light, as the canary vanished into the glass.

My mouth dropped open. This wasn't happening. It couldn't be real. Behind me the closet was deathly still. I whirled around. There on the rods were one hundred moonlit dresses: lifeless pieces of cloth.

I turned back. A ghostly canary shone in the glass of the moonlit window. What had I done? I'd made the closet go back to sleep. I'd lost the canary—the magical canary owned by the Queens of Eliora. Tears welled up in my eyes.

How would I ever get him back?

22

The sun mocked me, bathing the morning in an amber glow. The azure sky glistened with a supercilious air as if sniggering behind a cloud at me for raining all over my previous night's plans. Even the bristles in my hairbrush taunted me, snarling their sharp spikes in my hair. I could almost hear the dragons on the roof humming with amusement.

"Laundry day," Francesca sang out.

Tossing the brush aside, I put my crumpled wad of soiled clothes in the basket. Normally, I loved laundry day and the fresh clothes that came with it. But today I stuffed a roll in my clean apron pocket. What difference would a few crumbs make to a Walking Disaster?

I had to fix this somehow. One day, Princess Mariposa would want her canary back and Cherice would tell me to fetch him. Then what? I could tell the Princess the truth: that I opened the cage and let the bird out. But I couldn't look her in the eye and lie. I couldn't say that he flew away. And I couldn't say that he was stuck in the window.

No one would believe that.

I hung around the dormitory until the other girls filed out. Then I yanked the crate stamped ARTICHOKES out from under my bed and ripped off the cover.

"Iago, I need help. Something terrible happened—" I sputtered to a stop.

Inside the box, on a bed of pale sand, lay five white mice all curled up. I traced Iago's tail with my finger. *Plaster*. Iago and his family had turned back to plaster like they'd been when they were part of the frieze on the wall. Plaster! Yesterday, Iago and his children had been free. And now they weren't. Somehow, their freedom was linked to the canary. Thinking back, I realized I'd never met Iago until after I put the canary in Queen Candace's closet. The bird's singing woke up the closet and the mice. If I'd left the canary in its cage, Iago would still be free.

I eased the lid back in place and slid it under the bed. No sense taking Iago anywhere. I couldn't put him back in the frieze, and plaster had a nasty habit of breaking. I couldn't bear one more thing on my conscience.

Roger was right: I should have stayed in the under-cellar, where I belonged.

I hauled myself down to the pressing room and ironed my mountain of sheets. Lindy whistled as she worked, spots of color blooming on her cheeks. The sun shone. The morning passed. Somewhere Prince Baltazar crept closer to his prized talisman and I was powerless to stop him. I shoveled down my lunch and then whizzed through the last of my chores as Lindy waltzed into her cloak.

Broom in hand, I, Darling Dimple, Ex-Dragon-Thwarter, watched her go.

"You're looking pale, my dear," Cherice said, poking her head in the door after Lindy left. "You need sun."

"Yes, ma'am," I agreed, standing in a pool of sunlight. "I'll go see if I can find some."

She blinked and then shrugged. "So you should." She disappeared with a wave. To make sure she was gone, I counted under my breath . . . ninety-seven, ninety-eight, ninety-nine . . . which reminded me that once upon a time, there had been a hundred dresses. Before Darling the Disaster got ahold of them. I sighed. I could always take a second look at the window. I might think of something. Maybe there was a hidden catch or a trick pane in the glass.

That sounded stupid even to me, but it was worth a try.

The wardrobe hall was deserted. The door to Queen Candace's closet creaked as I pushed it open. A still room greeted me. The glass canary shone in the window. I ran a hand all around the window frame: on the top, the sides, and the curved groove underneath. Nothing.

"I'm sorry," I told the glass canary. "I ruined everything, didn't I? And now you're . . ."

What? Dead? Stuck? Gone? I ran my fingers over the splinters of yellow glass. Warmth caressed my skin. I pressed my palm into the window. A deep thrumming vibrated under my hand. A throbbing like a giant heartbeat in the glass itself. I closed my eyes and let my heart beat with the castle. And deep down under the thrumming, I felt a trickle of something like music, but also like a sizzle, as if something hot had singed the very tippy-tips of my fingers.

And then it rushed through me in a wave: magic, gallons and gallons of magic pouring through me, coloring my thoughts and filling me with delight. I felt the flicker of the canary's tail and the brooding of the gryphons. The mice squeaked. Birds twittered. Lions rumbled. They pulsed with life. And magic. Every animal in the castle from plaster to brass to marble pulsed with the castle's magic. It reached out and welcomed me in.

Like it *knew* me. It hovered around me, tickling my ears with a thousand voices. Fragments of words and phrases came to me all in a jumble. It wanted to tell me things, but it said too much, too quickly, like a choir all singing different songs. My ears buzzed. My head throbbed. My heart pounded.

And then a wisp of clear, bright magic beckoned me.

I followed it. Through the walls, the floors, the roofs, touching and sensing each creature in its web until I felt something cold. Leathery. Bitter. Something that pulsed with hate and snapped at me with sharp teeth.

I wrenched my hand back from the window, gasping.

The dragons knew it was me. They knew. They hated me and everyone else in the castle. They couldn't wait to break loose. They'd waited a long time for their revenge. And they meant to have it.

I scrubbed my palm on my apron, rubbing away the sensation of those teeth.

The canary was alive inside the castle's web of magic. All I had to do was set him free. *Somewhere* there had to be an answer. King Richard must have left some hint. In a book, a window, a painting . . . something I could see. He had to have because the magic was too big and too important for him to not have done so.

I had to find it.

I flung myself out of the closet and straight into the path of Francesca, fist clenched at her side. She wore a triumphant smile as if *she* had the world's greatest prize in her hand.

"I've been looking for you," she said in a timbre that echoed her mother's.

"I've been working," I said, eyeing the exit. Trust Francesca to keep the castle's only Dragon-Thwarter from her mission.

"I found something in the laundry." Her smile widened.

"Dirty clothes?" I guessed. "A piece of Gloria's secret candy stash stuck to someone's sock?"

"This." Francesca brought her hand up and unfurled her grip to reveal an iron key.

23

The key glinted darkly on the polished surface of the Head Steward's desk. I stood, hands clasped behind my back, wishing I'd thought to empty my pockets. Francesca bobbed on her toes like a ball that can't stop bouncing.

The Head Steward picked up the key and examined it. His medals tinkled faintly as his shoulders moved. I wrinkled my nose, resisting the urge to sneeze at the scent of lemon polish wafting off the desktop. The bookcase reeked of leather and old paper. A vase of roses sat on the mantelpiece; a medley of smoke, fragrance, and ashes seeped into the room. It wasn't a small room, but it felt tight—from the bulging bookcases to the heavily upholstered chairs to the tall glass-fronted armoire filled with keys.

Keys—hundreds of them, small, large, brass, silver, gold-plated, and iron—hung in ordered rows, tagged with different-colored tassels. I saw the empty hook where the iron key had hung. My chest tightened; the air squeezed out of my lungs. Spots swam before my eyes.

I blinked rapidly and caught the Head Steward's gaze, eyes bright under heavy brows.

"In the laundry?" he said, leaning back. His leather chair creaked.

"In Darling's apron!" Francesca pounced. "And I knew it was my duty—"

"Yes," the Head Steward said, "thank you, Francesca, you may go."

Francesca's lips wiggled like worms on a hook; she bounced from foot to foot. The Head Steward raised an eyebrow and Francesca, frowning, curtsied and left. He waited until the door closed behind her, then he eyed me again with that bright blue stare.

"How did this key find its way into your pocket?"

I twisted my fingers behind my back. "I picked it up and put it there."

"Picked it up? Where?"

"It was lying on a stairstep." I eyed my boots. I felt as dizzy as I had standing on the narrow crossbeam of the north roof. One false step, one wrong word, and I would plunge myself, Gillian, and Roger into serious trouble.

"And where *precisely* was this stairstep?" the Head Steward asked.

I looked up. "I didn't take that key, sir. I found it on a stair in the north wing and I put it in my pocket, and then I just forgot about it."

The Head Steward waited, polishing the key with his thumb.

"I meant to—to—" My chest contracted, ribs squeezing my heart like a vise.

He raised an eyebrow. *I meant to give it back;* the lie stung my tongue like a wasp. I'd meant to keep it and under that piercing gaze, I couldn't claim otherwise.

"I—I didn't take that key," I said.

He settled more comfortably in his chair. "The thing is, Darling, I believe you. You didn't take that key, but I think you know who did."

The words *a Messenger Boy* trembled on my lips, but I couldn't say them. If I did, then I'd have to explain how I knew. I'd have to snitch on Roger and Gillian.

"Taking the Princess's property is stealing. Even taking something you mean to put back is theft. Because once you pick it up"—he leaned forward, brandishing the key—"you intend to do something with it that you don't have the Princess's permission to do."

I gulped.

"Do you know what door this key opens?" His eyes bored into mine.

"The roof," I whispered unwillingly.

"Have you been up on the roof?"

I stared at my feet, afraid that if I looked up, I'd tell him everything.

His chair creaked again. "Darling, did you know that you should have gone to the orphanage when you were born?"

I shook my head. "No, Jane took care of me, she would never—"

"Never have sent you to the orphanage? No, she wouldn't. She begged. Let her keep you, and she would be responsible for you."

I blinked back tears. I never knew that Jane begged to keep me; I thought she did it because she had to.

"So, that still stands. She is responsible for you and for what you do."

My head whipped up. "But Jane had nothing to do with this!"

He shrugged. "You are suspended from the Princess's service until further notice. You can go explain yourself to Jane. She can decide what to do with you."

My eyes welled up. "I didn't take it! I swear it wasn't me!"

He took out his handkerchief and began shining up the key. "Then who did?"

I bit my lower lip.

"Whoever used this key could have fallen and been killed," the Head Steward said, rising. He walked across the room, unlocked the armoire, and returned the key to its hook.

24

I dried my eyes on the tea towel the Head Cook had laid on my knees. She worked with her back to me, searching her thick recipe books. She tapped her toe as she flipped pages, her broad back crisscrossed with apron strings, her hair bun dusted with flour. She'd parked me on the bench after I'd arrived distraught and unable to explain my sudden appearance. The bustle of the kitchens flowed around me. Orders rang out. Choppers and Slicers, Roasters and Bakers hurried about their business. A thousand rich aromas competed for my attention.

I had no place to go. I, Darling Nothing, had no home, no position, and no family. There was only Jane, who was unaware of what a wretched failure she'd raised. How would I ever face her?

If I hadn't let the canary out, then I wouldn't have forgotten about the key. If I'd given it back to Roger in the first place, then he'd be the one in trouble. Not me. He'd lose his job.

I twisted the soggy towel; I didn't want that to happen. I almost *liked* Roger. Well, I liked him enough that I didn't want to see him fired. Or Gillian. They were my friends. At least they used to be.

The Pastry Chef slid a plate holding a jam tart onto my knees. "Eat something; you're making us all depressed."

"Food can't cure every ill," the Head Cook commented.

"Well, it should!" the Pastry Chef shot back. "Eat that," he told me, and marched off.

The Head Cook glanced at me over her broad shoulder. Her gray eyes twinkled. "I've never known you to take as much as a grape without asking. Keys are an odd item with which to start one's life of crime. I'd have thought cakes more likely."

I blinked. "How did you know about the key?"

"Oh, Darling, everyone knows. There are few secrets among the Under-staff." She wagged a finger at me. "You'll always be one of us. It doesn't matter what uniform you wear; you were one of us first."

My eyes watered afresh.

"Now eat that tart. We don't waste good food in *my* kitchens."

I swallowed my tears and took a bite. A burst of cherry jam exploded on my tongue. I gobbled the pastry up and wiped my mouth off with the sodden towel. Food might not cure every ill, but that tart did me good.

"I didn't take the key," I said.

"Course not. But Marsdon thinks you know who did," she said.

Marsdon. Only someone as important as the Head Cook would call the Head Steward by name. "I think," she said as if her opinion were the one that mattered, "that there are only ten people who could have taken that key." She ticked them off on her fingers. "Me, Marsdon, Pepper-whistle, Esteban the Head Footman, or"—she winked at me—"one of the Messenger Boys."

"I really don't know who took it," I said.

"Oh," she said, waving this away, "it makes no difference to me who did. Some old key that opens some door no one uses. *Bah.* It's not like the key to the Princess's jewel case. Marsdon ought to send the guilty party to bed without supper and have done with it."

"Do you think that's all that will happen?" I asked, hope rising. Maybe Roger and Gillian weren't in as much trouble as I'd thought.

Before she could answer, the Under-servants began streaming in for supper. Gillian trailed in at the back of the line, scowling at me. A stab of anger struck me; my tears dried up. How dare she scowl at me after she'd gotten me in such trouble? The other Under-servants eyed me with a mixture of awe and suspicion. I looked away, inching to the edge of the bench. Maybe I should go look for Jane.

The Supreme Scrubstress loomed over me, her lips curled in a frown, swaying on her tiny feet. Her wooden-handled sponge was nowhere to be seen, but my backside twitched anyway.

"I gave you the opportunity of a lifetime!" she barked. "Under-presser to the Princess!" Her double chin quivered. "And you threw it away!"

"I didn't take it!" The words squeaked out of me.

"Darling didn't take it." The Head Cook slammed her recipe book shut. "Don't *you* say she did," she said in the blistering voice she saved for Cooks who ruined sauces.

With a startled squawk, the Supreme Scrubstress collapsed on the bench beside me. Spoons stopped in midair as the Under-servants gaped. The Supreme Scrubstress wasn't a woman to be easily vanquished. The Head Cook turned back to her notes. Across the room, a guilty flush crept across Gillian's face.

"Jane was right," Marci mumbled. "I shouldn't have said anything about the roof."

"Oh!" the wail sailed over the bent heads of the Under-servants as Jane entered. "Darling, what have you done?"

I shrank against Marci. With one hand, Jane clutched her heart—as if I'd broken it—and with the other she felt her way across the room. A sob rose in my throat; I'd hurt Jane, Jane who'd begged to keep me, Darling Dimple, Traitor.

"I hope you're happy," Marci said, poking me in the ribs.

Jane whirled on the Supreme Scrubstress. "If you hadn't dared me to go up on that roof, then none of this would have happened, Marci!"

Marci shot up off the bench. "Me? You broke my very best doll—given to me by Queen Paloma!"

The two glared at each other over my head.

"You had more than your share of fancy toys, Marci," the Head Cook commented.

"But that doll was made out of porcelain, with real hair!" the Supreme Scrubstress exclaimed. "She dropped it down the stairs! On purpose!"

"You bragged!" Jane shot back. "You were the Queen's favorite."

"You were jealous!" Marci said.

"You were selfish!"

"Crosspatch!"

"Daydreamer!"

"You dared me!" Jane shouted. "If I hadn't looked that dragon in the eye, I'd still have my sight!"

Marci's face crumpled. "I just wanted to scare you. I didn't mean for that to happen."

Jane's shoulders slumped. "I'm sorry I broke your doll." She flopped on the bench next to me. "I didn't really mean to, but I was so angry. I never had any and you had lots and you'd never let me play with one. Just one, Marci. It didn't have to be the best one."

Marci sank heavily down on my other side. "I never meant for you to lose your sight," she said, dabbing her mouth with her handkerchief.

"I wanted to be an Icer like Aunt Doris and decorate cakes," Jane said, sniffling.

"I wanted to be the Wardrobe Mistress, like my grand-mother," Marci said with a sigh.

I sat squeezed between the two of them. The dragons had stolen Jane's eyesight and she'd never even told me about it. Well, there were lots of things she'd never told me. I didn't know she begged to keep me or that she and Marci had been such close friends. Or that the castle was full of magic.

"Look at us," Jane said. "I'm a half-blind Picker and you're stuck in the under-cellar."

Marci nodded, a tear rolling down her cheek. "We had such dreams."

Jane reached over to squeeze Marci's hand. "We've paid the price for our foolishness."

"I should never, ever have told you the *magic word,*" Marci whispered. "I never meant to hurt you; you were my best friend!"

"Oh, Marci, you idiot, you're still my best friend," Jane wailed, and threw her arms around Marci's shoulders.

The two sobbed on each other's necks. The air rushed out of my lungs as they crushed me. My thoughts whirled. There was a magic word! It roused the dragon enough to injure Jane's eyesight. It didn't free the dragon, but it woke it somehow. There was more than just the talisman—there was a magic word!

A hand reached between the two and yanked me free.

"There you are!" Lindy said, shaking me. "There's work to do."

She waved a folded parchment under my nose.

"Leave off, she's been suspended," the Head Cook said, grabbing my arm.

"She's mine!" Lindy said, pulling on the other. "And I've got the paper to prove it."

"Let me see that," the Head Cook said, snatching the paper.

"Let Darlin' see," Lindy said, grabbing it back and shoving it at me.

I took the parchment. It was cream-colored and had a glob of red wax pressed to it.

"Read it aloud, Darlin'," Lindy said.

I read:

I hereby order the reinstatement of Darling Dimple,
Under-presser, to My service and decree that this
Dreadful Misunderstanding never be mentioned again.
As My Key is recovered, I instruct My Head Steward to
consider the matter closed.

Signed,
Princess Mariposa

The paper shook in my hand.

"Well," Lindy said, "what do you say to that?"

"Um, oh," I mumbled, dazed.

"Thanks would be in better order." The Head Cook nudged me. "However did you manage this, Lindy?"

"Manage it? You don't expect me to give up the best Under-presser I've ever had! I went straight to Marsdon and gave him a piece of my mind. Told me he couldn't reinstate her without the Princess's sayin' so. Well, there!" She jabbed at the parchment. "The Princess says so."

"You went to the Princess for me?" I gasped. The words *best Under-presser I've ever had* echoed in my ears.

Lindy blushed.

"Th-thank you," I said.

"You left a pack of work behind you, girl!" Lindy said, tossing her hair over her shoulder.

Princess Mariposa had saved me. Lindy had stood up for me. Jane had begged to keep me. And the Head Cook had said I was one of them. It was too much. I broke down and bawled.

"Someone should feed that child supper," I heard the Pastry Chef grumble.

25

Francesca shoved me aside at the mirror the next morning. "Out of my way," she snarled.

Sparks flew from the bristles as she brushed them through her hair. Evidently, she'd thought she was rid of me after she found the key.

Smothering a smile, I tied my hair back with a ribbon. It wouldn't last long, but I did it anyway. The other girls tiptoed around, hurrying to get dressed before she noticed them. Cowards.

I took my time getting ready, letting Francesca see that I did.

"Hurry up," she said. "Her Highness can't wait all day."

"Her Highness isn't waiting for me; Lindy is, because she told the Princess I was the best Under-presser she'd ever had."

I didn't bother to point out that her sister, Faustine, wasn't the best ever. I smiled at her instead, a great big sunny smile.

Francesca's fingers curled into claws. I made a point of glancing at my hairbrush to see that it was glue-free. And then I rubbed the toe of my boot on the glossy, sand-free floor. Francesca quivered like a too-tight laundry line plucked by clothespins.

"Have a nice day," I said as I left.

I heard a *thwack* as something hit the closed door behind me. Goodness, if she threw her brush any harder, she'd break it. The thought made me smile all over again.

At the pressing room, Lindy whistled while she worked.

"Morning, Darlin', there's a pile of towels for you," she said, dancing her iron over a delicate lace ruffle like a bee flitting over a flower.

"Sure thing," I said, heating my irons.

How could Lindy plot the dragons' release one moment and rescue me the next? It didn't make sense. Could she be rotten at heart and still be kind? Or was she pretending? I had to know.

Following Lindy's lead, I zipped my iron over those towels, stinging the wrinkles out and buzzing them into a folded pile. I whizzed and spun my way through all my work, finishing just as Lindy swirled her cloak around her square shoulders.

"Have a spot of lunch," she said.

I nodded, strolling along after her. I followed her as far as I could without being obvious. At the turn to the kitchens, I paused and said, "I wonder what's for lunch?"

"Save some for the others," Lindy said with a laugh, and headed off.

"I'll try," I called after her. Then I ducked around a corner.

I, Darling Dimple, Intrepid Scout, would track the Black-Cloaked Tigress. My heart ached at the thought of Lindy pursuing mischief against the Princess, but Prince Baltazar *had* to be stopped at all costs.

Lindy walked to the edge of the kitchens. There on a table sat a basket with a checked cloth bundled up inside it. Lindy snatched it off the table and tucked it under her long cloak.

A tantalizing whiff of fresh bread set my stomach rumbling.

Was the Baker in on Lindy's scheming?

Lindy strolled purposefully on. She rounded a corner and shot up a short flight of stairs to a door that opened on a courtyard. The courtyard acted like a bridge between the entrance to the stables and upper eastern lawns. I waited until Lindy crossed it and then I ventured out. The gate on the far side swung shut as I bounded across.

Over the gate, I heard Lindy hail a Guard. I shrank into

a sliver of shadow. *Boom, boom, boom.* My heart pounded. I pressed my hand to my chest to still it before it gave me away.

I peeked between the gate slats. The Guard grinned at Lindy.

"Looking for the Captain?" he asked.

"Oh, he is on duty?" Lindy said. "I didn't know. Just out to take some air."

"You should take some air over by the east watch station," the Guard said with a laugh.

Lindy poked the man in his chest. "You should mind your post."

I gasped, but the Guard laughed and walked away. Lindy set off at a brisker pace. I scurried after her, waiting only long enough to be sure the Guard was facing the other way. She marched straight to the east watch station, a little building above the eastern terrace.

What business could Lindy have with the Captain of the Guards? Was *he* in on this too? Was everybody? Maybe I was the only loyal servant left. Well, me and Jane; I was sure Jane was loyal. And most of the Under-servants. I couldn't picture the Supreme Scrubstress involved in any tomfoolery.

I had to hear what went on inside that watch station. Glancing around, I sidled up to one of the station's open windows and huddled underneath.

I heard laughter and smelled bread. I wormed up to the windowsill, eager for a peek.

Lindy had thrown off her cloak and was slicing a loaf of mouthwateringly crusty bread with a dagger—the sort the Guards carried. Standing over her was Captain Bryce. He was handsome in his blue uniform, taller than Lindy and even more square-shouldered.

"You'll fatten me up, sweetheart," he said, patting his midsection.

Sweetheart?

Lindy laughed. "I brought some orange marmalade, sausages, and cake."

"Oh," he pretended to groan, but his eyes lit up.

"Guard duty is hungry work," she said.

"You spoil me," he told her, and pulled her close.

I ducked under the sill, gagging. *Kissing?* I had expected Lindy to rendezvous with Prince Baltazar, not Captain Bryce. That's what the note said. Wasn't it?

Meet me tonight at the base of the western tower.—B

I'd thought that meant Baltazar, but what if . . . there was a watch station at the western tower. Maybe Lindy had gone there to meet Captain Bryce. That would explain how she stayed dry and why Prince Baltazar was saying good night to the Princess instead of being outside with Lindy.

Maybe Lindy wasn't the Cloaked Lady. Maybe it was someone else.

A shadow fell over my face. I glanced up, blinking in the sunlight.

Roger the Freckled Wonder stood over me.

"What are you doing here?" he asked.

I struggled up from the ground, dusting my skirt off. "Nothing."

"Hey, Roger," Captain Bryce called through the window. "Is that your girlfriend?"

Roger's freckles vanished in a blaze of scarlet. "It's just Darling," he spat out.

Lindy poked her head out the window. "Darlin'?"

"Yes, ma'am," I said as if nothing unusual were going on.

"What are you doing out there?" Lindy asked.

"Um," I said. "Talking to Roger."

He glared at me.

Lindy's brow furrowed. "Did you have lunch?"

"No, ma'am, I was just going."

"The kitchen is that way," she said, pointing.

"Yes, ma'am."

"Of all the places to talk," she muttered, pulling her head back in the window.

"Well," Captain Bryce said, "it doesn't require a key."

Roger's mouth popped open in a look of absolute horror.

I wanted to die right then and there.

Captain Bryce laughed. "You two lovebirds scoot now and get your lunch."

26

I turned on my heel and made a beeline for the kitchens. I'd missed enough meals dragon-thwarting; I wanted my lunch. The breeze cooled my burning cheeks. *Lovebirds.* I shuddered.

"Darling," Roger called.

I whirled around, my fists tight.

Roger pulled off his cap and wiped his brow on his sleeve.

"What?"

"Is that why you didn't snitch on me? You think you're my *girlfriend*?" he asked, saying *girlfriend* as if he meant *dead rat*.

My blood boiled.

"I didn't snitch on you for the same reason I didn't snitch on Gillian," I told him. "I am not a snitch."

Roger's mouth opened and closed.

"And I'm not your girlfriend," I said. "I'm not even sure we're friends—*friends* don't let friends get suspended for keys *they* stole."

"Borrowed!" he shouted.

"The Head Steward didn't call it borrowing."

Roger slapped his cap back on his head. "You got one thing right. You and me ain't friends."

He stomped off.

I let him go, following at a safe distance. After all I'd been through, thwarting dragons, hiding, sneaking around trying to save the Princess, I figured I had a good solid meal coming to me. Roger or no Roger.

I marched into the kitchen, took my place in line behind some Upper-scrubbers, and ladled my plate full. I was so hungry I could have eaten half a cow. The Cook at the serving table eyed me as I reached for a second tart, but I dared her to object with a fierce scowl. She stirred the soup and pretended not to notice.

I saw Roger sitting with Gillian on the far side of the room. They saw me. Roger leaned over to whisper something to Gillian. So I walked across the room and sat in a corner at an empty table. Anger bubbled through my veins. All I'd wanted was a nice little adventure, one that ended before bedtime. One that didn't leave scars or cost me anything. Was that too much to ask?

I shoved my food into my mouth, not tasting a bite. I looked daggers at anyone who wandered too close to my table. No one else sat down. Fine with me. I didn't want company. When I was finished, I dumped my dish in the washtub and stalked out.

Lovebirds. Bah. I wouldn't like Roger if he was the last boy in the whole castle. I stomped up the servants' stairs. It was a long hike back to the pressing room. I nursed my indignation as I walked. Lovebirds! I'd rather kiss a pig than Roger. I'd rather marry a toad. The stone gryphon outside the pressing room window made a better friend. I could at least count on it to be there.

A sudden tear darted down my cheek. I swatted it away.

"My dear," Cherice said as I entered the wardrobe hall, "such a face! Has Francesca done something?"

"No," I said.

"Indeed," Cherice said, sorting through a pile of ribbons.

"Cherice, did you know that Lindy has a sweetheart?"

"The brave Captain?" She smiled. "Yes, our Lindy is smitten indeed."

"Are you sure?" I asked.

"About Lindy?" Cherice said, smoothing a crimson ribbon. "She sneaks off to see him every chance she gets. Some Cook supplies her with picnics. She thinks she

conceals them under that cloak, but there are eyes everywhere. Soon the Captain shall be all fattened up and have
to retire to some farm."

"Farm? Why?"

"My dear, one simply cannot have one's Captain of the
Guards be less than athletic. It does not do. He must be
ready at all times to fight for the Princess!"

My brow knit. I felt like I was hanging from the castle
roof by the tips of my fingers, the ground swimming below
me, beckoning. Lindy wasn't the Cloaked Lady.

Who was?

Cherice took my chin in her hand. "Did you have your
heart set on the gallant Guard?" Her eyes twinkled with
amusement.

"No!" I said, appalled. "I don't have my heart set on
anyone!"

"Hmm," she said. "The heart has its own mind in these
matters."

"Does Lindy want to live on a farm?"

Cherice shuddered. "Evidently."

Her gown strained across her shoulders as she sorted.
The little magnifying glass she wore on a long chain swung
to and fro as she moved. I studied it as it swung: it was an
oval crystal with a faceted edge, not the sort of glass used
in magnifiers. Cherice always wore it. I wondered where
she'd gotten it.

"Would you like to marry and settle down on a farm?"
I asked.

Her eyes flew open. "Goodness! No." She tapped her
magnifying glass against her slender side. "I was not born
for tending pigs."

Cherice selected a carved wooden case out of a pile.
She unlocked the case and lifted the lid. Inside, a tiara
glistened on a bed of satin. Cherice lifted it out gently and
held it out to me.

"See? Is it not magnificent?"

The gold of the tiara formed the outline of two swans,
whose arched necks made an open heart shape. A glowing
heart-shaped ruby nestled between the two swans.

"Oh my."

Cherice settled the tiara in her own blond curls. "What
do you think?"

"It makes you beautiful," I said.

"One can be what one imagines, a farmer or a princess," Cherice murmured. "I have dressed princesses in
four kingdoms and one day, I too will—"

I cast a guilty look over my shoulder. What would Princess Mariposa say if she knew Cherice wore her tiara? I
rubbed my sweaty palms on my apron. Cherice noticed
and removed the tiara.

"Time to put it away," she said. "I thought you might
like to see it." She settled the tiara in its case and locked it.

"Thank you. I should be—"

"Here," Cherice said, scooping up the ribbons from her desktop. "Her Highness said to give these to her Girls. You can have first pick."

A stream of silk ribbons flowed across her palm: scarlet, azure, violet, sapphire, emerald, and silver among the colors.

"I couldn't choose," I said, wishing I could have them all and feeling like I didn't deserve even one. I'd failed Princess Mariposa.

"This one." Cherice selected a pale aquamarine. "It matches your eyes."

She laid the slender strip on my outstretched palm. It gleamed like an ocean wave on the pale sand of my skin.

"Does it really match my eyes?" I said.

"Indeed," Cherice answered.

She took the ribbon and tied it in a bow on the side of my head.

"Run, see," she suggested.

I ran to the pressing room mirror. The ribbon flashed gaily against my pale hair. My water-colored eyes reflected the shade of the ribbon. Aquamarine. I had aquamarine eyes. I stood a little straighter. Roger said they looked yellow. *He* didn't know anything.

27

Prince Baltazar had convinced Princess Mariposa to plant the butterfly bush seeds. Why wait until next spring? Plant them now. So they'd grow immediately. And they had. It wasn't long before they began to bloom.

Time was running out. I had to free the canary and wake up the dresses if I wanted to find the Cloaked Lady and unmask Prince Baltazar's scheme.

So every time Lindy visited her Captain, I scoured the castle for any clue that King Richard had left behind about the magic. I studied paintings and searched behind draperies and under furniture. I looked over every animal statue that I could get close to, hoping one of them would blink or sneeze or wiggle—something, for any hint that they were about to wake up and help me. Something had pulled these creatures into the castle's magic web. Something had to set them free. *Something.*

You had to give King Richard credit; he'd hidden his clues cleverly. I ran out of places I could search. I couldn't go into the west wing or the King's library. Maybe some old book lay there waiting to divulge all the King's secrets, but even if I found a way to peek inside, the library held thousands of volumes. I could never look through them all.

I took my search outdoors. I reasoned that since the starburst was the only spot where one could see the dragons, maybe the King had left other clues outside. After all, there were lots of animals in the gardens: bronze, marble, granite—maybe one of them could teach me something.

I started with my old friends, the bronze lions. They sat on their haunches, alert. Greenish tinges curled through their manes and crusted the tips of their claws, as if they'd been waiting too long to pounce and grown old and dusty. Their long shadows bounded down the stairs, enticing them to follow. But their burnished brown eyes remained welded to the horizon.

"Talk to me," I commanded them.

They didn't so much as twitch a whisker. So I searched them, from the crowns of their heads to the tassels of their tails. I plunked myself between one beast's front paws and curled up to think. Was the lion only metal? Or was it like

Iago, drawn in by the castle's magic? I knew the animals in the walls were alive; I'd felt them when I'd touched the window. But was the same true for the lawns? I rested my chin on my knees.

Heat from the lion soaked into my back. I yawned; that morning, I'd pressed an avalanche of sheets and towels, and then I'd helped Lindy clean and polish the irons. The warmth eased my aching shoulders. My eyelids fluttered.

"Your Grace," a man's voice said, "this message arrived this morning."

I snapped awake. A paper rustled. A hand tapped the head of the lion. I froze.

"Send word to Father," Prince Sterling said. I recognized his voice from the Ruby Luncheon. "I must have proof, and soon."

I crouched, ready to jump out and run away.

"As you wish," the other man replied. "I'll send a courier tonight."

I heard footsteps walk away on the paving stones. I exhaled. I stretched my cramped legs. Then I wriggled out from between the cleft in the lion's legs.

A hand caught me as I emerged. The same Footman who'd nodded to Prince Sterling on the landing that night held me in his viselike grip.

"What have we here?" he said.

He pulled me to my feet. I said nothing. I didn't answer

to Footmen. I had a right to be on the eastern lawns; all the servants did.

"Who are you?" I asked.

He shrugged, his muscles rippling under his jacket sleeve. "A Footman."

"I'm one of the Princess's Girls," I replied. Not that I was telling him anything my uniform hadn't already.

"What are you doing here?"

"Let go," I said, wiggling.

"What are you doing here?" he said, locking his fingers around my apron strap. "Why were you hiding?"

"You're hurting me," I wailed.

I heard tip-tapping steps hurrying toward us.

"See here," the Supreme Scrubstress said, rounding a hedge. "Turn her loose."

I'd never been so glad to see anyone in my entire life.

"He's hurting me," I told her. "Lindy said I could take a break—and he just *grabbed* me."

I twisted then, and my apron strap gave way with a loud *riiip*.

Startled, he released me. I inched away, rubbing my sore shoulder. My torn apron strap dangled down my front. Marci eyed the damage to my clothes with a growing frown.

"I want to know what she's doing out here," the Footman persisted.

Marci shook a finger at him.

"She's none of your business," she said, chins wagging. "Get back to your station before I tell Marsdon you're away."

The Footman glowered down at Marci, but she held her ground. I ducked behind her, as far out of the Footman's reach as possible. The Footman dusted off his sleeve and straightened his jacket. He gave me a look that said he'd better not run into me again.

"If the Head Housekeeper can't keep track of her girls, then it's no business of mine," he said. "Good day." He nodded, turned on his heel, and left.

The Supreme Scrubstress rounded on me, snatching me by the arm before I could scurry off.

"What are you doing out here?"

"T-taking a break," I said for lack of a better answer.

Her nostrils curled; her chins trembled. "Is Gillian out here with you?"

I shook my head no, glad that she'd changed the subject.

She held me for another moment, weighing my expression. And then she let me go.

"Get back upstairs. I have an Under-dryer to thrash."

I scampered out of there. I ran with my eyes peeled for that Footman. Who was he? And why was he sending messages for Prince Sterling? I'd thought Cherice had said that Prince Sterling was some impoverished prince from nowhere. Who, then, was his father? What proof did he need? And why the hurry to get it?

My brain vibrated like a hornet's nest stirred with a stick. Was Prince Sterling somehow involved in all this scheming? I liked him. I hated to believe that he too was rotten.

I stopped at the girls' dormitory to fetch a clean apron, tucking my damaged one under my arm. I'd get Cherice to help me fix it. Just as I walked into the wardrobe hall, the dressing room door flew open.

Cherice stood there, a glistening vermilion silk over her arm. "My dear, all your gowns become you," she said over her shoulder. "They are made for just that purpose."

Princess Mariposa came to the door in her petticoats, brow furrowed. "There is becoming and then there is *becoming*." She caught sight of my dangling apron strap. "Darling, what happened?"

I shrugged. "Just an accident."

"I'll find you a needle and thread," Cherice said. "Young ladies who have accidents do their own mending. Your Highness, I will find you another gown, one more becoming."

I gestured to the vermilion silk. "That's pretty."

"Yes, it is," Cherice responded, gritting her teeth. "Perfectly lovely."

"Oh, it is," Princess Mariposa agreed. "But not . . . just the thing for this evening."

"Of course not," Cherice muttered under her breath.

Princess Mariposa arched her eyebrow at that. A stubborn look settled into her features. "Come with me, Darling. You choose what I should wear."

"Me?" My every nerve thrilled at the thought.

"Of course you," she said. "Cherice, open closet six."

Inclining her head, Cherice walked over to closet six and unlocked the door. Throwing it open, she said in a cold voice, "There you go, Darling Dimple, Advisor to Her Highness, choose!"

I clutched my damaged apron. I'd made Cherice angry without meaning to.

"Come, don't be shy," the Princess urged.

Cherice waited at the door, a fixed smile on her lips. The Princess led me into the closet packed with ball gowns.

"I want something special for tonight," Princess Mariposa said.

I glanced up at her; her sapphire eyes flashed. Something special. A forest of gowns, a dizzying rainbow of color and fabric: velvet, satin, silk, brocade, jacquard, embroideries, jewels, ribbons surrounded me. *Something special.* I remembered Princess Mariposa standing in the flash of lightning, resembling a queen stepped down from the night sky. She'd looked like a fairy-tale princess. She needed that sort of dress.

I searched while Cherice tapped her toe impatiently. Wedged between a sea-green chiffon and a salmon tapestry glimmered a fold of blue-white satin. I eased the satin out from between the other dresses. A glistening white dress slithered into my hands, a crystal-encrusted silvery-white dream like a shaft of starlight illuminating the closet. The bodice was fitted and sleeveless, flaring from its crystal-encased waist to its reams of silvery-white skirt.

"This one," I said, holding it out to her.

"It is not the season for white, my dear," Cherice said over the Princess's shoulder. "Choose another, something colorful."

"I forgot about this dress," Princes Mariposa said. She caressed the glimmering satin.

"You'll look like a star shining in the dark," I said.

"That sea green—" Cherice began.

"A star shining in the dark," the Princess repeated, bemused. "I'll try it on."

Taking the dress, she hurried out of the closet toward her dressing room.

With an exasperated grimace, Cherice hastened after her. I followed, drawn like a moth to a flame. I slipped into the dressing room uninvited, holding my breath. The Princess stepped into the silvery-white gown, holding it against her chest.

"Hurry," she said. "Lace me up."

Cherice threaded the laces on the bodice's back, pulling them tight and tying them into a bow before tucking them in the back of the dress. The Princess put her hands on her hips, settling the dress where she wanted it. Then she turned to look in the mirror.

"I'll want silver slippers and—" She wet her lips, studying herself in the mirror.

The silvery-white darkened her hair to blue-black and made her pale skin pink in comparison. Her sapphire eyes gleamed; her ruby lips glistened. She glowed with the reflected light of the crystals. She sparkled like starlight.

"Diamonds!" I exclaimed.

Cherice glared at me.

"Shoo," she hissed. She turned to the Princess. "My dear, it is not at all the thing for late summer."

"Diamonds!" Princess Mariposa echoed. "Oh, yes! Fetch them."

Cherice stiffened her spine. "As you wish," she said, and stalked off.

"Oh, Darling, this will be a night to remember." Princess Mariposa spun on the tips of her toes. Her skirts billowed and the crystals flashed. Roses bloomed on her cheeks.

She stopped and held a hand to her forehead. "Oh my, this is laced tightly. Open a window, please."

I hurried to the windows and cranked one open. A breeze flowed in, followed by a little garnet butterfly. The butterfly flitted up and down, drifting up to settle on the top of a curtain rod.

Cherice hurried back carrying a necklace and a pair of slippers. Cherice placed the slippers on the floor and the Princess stepped into them. Then Cherice draped the necklace about the Princess's neck and fastened the clasp. Diamonds glittered like dewdrops against her skin.

"There!" Princess Mariposa said, fingering the diamonds. "Is this not perfect?"

"Yes, my dear, it is very special. A trifle off-season, but—"

Princess Mariposa spread her hands. "Is this not perfect?" she demanded.

Before Cherice could reply, the butterfly flew down and settled on the Princess's outstretched hand. She gasped but held still.

"Look," she whispered.

The garnet butterfly had a brown body and a ruffle of caramel around its wings. On each fluttering wing were set two eyes ringed in black: one yellow and vibrant blue, the other blue and copper.

"An *Inachis io*, a peacock," Princess Mariposa breathed

in wonder. "Oh, Cherice, a peacock butterfly. These are so rare. And here it is, right here."

"It's beautiful," I said, ducking to see the rainbow of colors on the underside of its wings.

"I've always, *always* wanted one," the Princess said.

I winced, thinking of all the butterflies pinned in the butterfly room.

"It will make a nice addition to your collection," Cherice said, and cupped her hands to capture it.

Princess Mariposa squealed. "Don't touch it!"

As if aware of Cherice's intent, the butterfly rose and flew out the open window.

Princess Mariposa watched it go. "This is a sign," she said.

"That Your Highness has chosen the right dress?" Cherice asked with a hint of irritation.

"The bushes bloom and the one butterfly I've always wanted appears," Princess Mariposa said to herself, as if neither of us was there. "It's a sign. It *is* true love."

Cherice glowed with delight. "Oh, it is, my dear. It is!"

Those stupid seeds! I *knew* they were trouble.

"Maybe it's just a coincidence," I protested.

"Thank you for your help," Princess Mariposa murmured, and glided off to dinner like a sleepwalker.

28

The next morning the herald announced the engagement of Mariposa Celesta Regina Valentina, Princess Royal of Eliora, to Prince Baltazar of Candala. The castle exploded in an outburst of celebration. At long last, the Princess had found her true love. Halls rang with singing. Every corner of the castle shone with polish, every face beamed, and every day dawned brighter than the last.

Every heart rejoiced except mine. I, Darling the Wretched, hunched over my irons and worked in silent misery, the only one in the castle aware of the doom lurking over our heads. I had failed completely. I'd failed the dresses, the canary, the Princess, and the entire kingdom.

I thought things couldn't get any worse, but I was

wrong. Princess Mariposa set an early autumn date for the wedding. She ordered the King's regalia brought out to be cleaned. And then she wanted her canary back.

My heart fell to my boots at the news.

"Wh-what?" My knees knocked together. "She wants *what*?"

"Her canary, silly," Cherice said. She tugged playfully on my ribbon. "Just put it back before the Princess dresses for dinner." Then she turned and vanished in a swirl of skirts.

My legs collapsed. I landed on the floor, a puddle of abject despair.

Vividly I pictured Princess Mariposa's astonishment turn into rage as I cowered before her. How dare I open the canary's cage? How dare I lose him?

Darling the Careless. Darling the Thoughtless. Darling the Ungrateful.

What could I do? Where could I turn? Who could save me?

Who indeed? There was only one person I could turn to now.

The wooden stairs creaked underneath me. The smell of fires burning tickled my nose. With each step, the rising heat warmed my skin. A sheen of moisture clung to the walls. Except for the hiss of steaming water and the crackle of fire, the under-cellar echoed with silence. The Scrubbers, Dryers, and Laundresses were up in the kitchens enjoying their lunch.

Above, a stair groaned as someone bounced on it.

"What are you doing here?" Gillian asked behind me.

I shrugged. "Looking for the Head Scrubber."

"Ooh, she's the *Head Scrubber* now, is she?" Gillian said.

"She always was," I replied, too dispirited to argue with her.

Gillian squinted at me. "Why are you really here? Get let go?"

"Nope. Just want to talk to her," I replied.

Gillian pulled a soggy sponge out of her soiled apron pocket. "Want to make some bubbles? Like old times?"

Her heart-shaped face pinked with hope. Her eyes sparkled. A dimple creased her cheeks. I could have told her a whopper: all about a queen and a closet full of magic dresses. I was tempted to tell her everything. But I only had until dinner and, once I started talking, I wasn't sure I'd ever be able to stop.

"I can't, sorry," I said. "I've got to go."

"Oh." She stuffed the sponge back in her pocket, forcing a trickle of water to soak her skirt. Then she stepped off the last step and walked away without looking back.

The Supreme Scrubstress had a bedroom upstairs with the other important servants, but like the Head Steward, she also had an office. Of sorts. At the end of the long line of hearths and scrubbing stations sat a narrow alcove. Years ago, someone had braced the alcove's heavy ceiling timbers with an extra set of pillars. A red-checked curtain hung from a rope strung between them. I hovered outside the curtain, biting my lip.

"Who's there?" the Supreme Scrubstress called.

"It's Darling. May I come in?"

A plump hand batted the fabric aside. The Supreme Scrubstress peered out at me, sharp-eyed and suspicious.

"You're a sorry sight," she said. "What's wrong?"

"I need help, and you're the only person who can help me," I said.

Her eyes widened in surprise. "Me? What help could I be?"

"It's about the canary," I whispered.

"Come in," she said, holding the curtain aside.

I squeezed past her. The office surprised me. Thick carpet squished underfoot. An old sofa sat in the corner, lined with embroidered pillows. A collection of drawings of scenic vistas and faraway places hung on the walls. It looked like a room belonging to someone with an imagination, someone who longed for more than just the undercellar.

"Sit down and tell me about it," the Supreme Scrubstress said, sinking into the sofa and gesturing to a stool.

I parked myself on the stool. Where did I begin?

"Several weeks ago, the Princess became annoyed with her canary," I said. "Cherice told me to find somewhere to keep him until she asked for him back."

The Supreme Scrubstress's eyes gleamed as she traced a pattern on the arm of the sofa with her forefinger.

"I didn't know where to take him, and so I just put him in the closet."

"Which closet?" the Supreme Scrubstress asked in a low voice.

"Queen Candace's. Because it was unlocked and I thought no one would care," I answered, squirming on the hard stool.

At *Candace*, she traced faster with her finger.

"So?" she said as if we were discussing the weather.

"Remember how you said that there was a story that the canary was the same one owned by Queen Candace and that he was magic?"

"I suggest," she said, standing up, "that you go back to work and stop talking nonsense."

"I tried on a dress," I said, desperate to keep her listening.

"You what?" she hissed in a hoarse whisper.

I leaned forward, anxious to say this in as quiet a tone as possible. "I. Tried. On. A. Dress. Candace's dress. When the canary was in the closet."

Perspiration coated her forehead. She fanned herself, the rolls around her middle jiggling as if agitated. And then it dawned on me. It was so obvious. I couldn't believe I hadn't figured it out before.

"You tried on the dresses, too, didn't you?" I said. "When you were little and you visited your grandmother and she was busy with Queen Paloma's wardrobe and you had the canary, you put on a dress and you *looked in the mirror!*"

The Supreme Scrubstress's face turned white. She collapsed on the sofa.

I clapped my hand over my mouth at the audacity of it all. She'd done it too!

Her chest heaved. Her hand groped under the pillows, and then she pulled out a fan and started vigorously fanning herself. Her bun began to disintegrate, strands of gray-streaked hair sliding down.

I didn't say any more. She'd turned a bad shade of green and I was scared she'd drop over dead.

Gradually her breathing slowed and so did her fanning. She dug a handkerchief out of her sleeve and mopped her face. She ran her tongue around her dry lips, moistening them.

"What have you done?" she asked.

That was a big question. It occurred to me that I'd done a lot, much more than I wanted to admit to. Besides, it was getting late. The sounds of washing and scrubbing filtered through the curtain: everyone was back at work, the afternoon was wearing on.

"I opened the cage and the canary flew around. Then he just *popped* back into the stained-glass bird on the closet window," I blurted out. "He's gone. Princess Mariposa's asked for him back and I have until dinnertime and I don't know how to get him out of there."

"Why are you asking me about this?" the Supreme Scrubstress asked, her color returning.

"Because you know about the canary and you know things about the castle and you know"—my voice dropped to a ghost of a whisper—"the magic word."

She swallowed like someone caught stealing.

"There are things you don't understand, dangerous things, things not meant to be tampered with," she said.

"I know, things like looking at the dragons and saying—" My mouth hung open, my words lost in midair. I saw it—SARVINDER—engraved on the golden collar. That was it. It wasn't a name, it was a magic word! Jane said it and it hurt her eyesight. But she said it to the dragon. What would happen if I said it to the canary?

The Supreme Scrubstress clamped her hand over my mouth. "Don't say it!"

I shook my head to indicate that I wouldn't. She eased

her hand away, ready to slap it back on in a moment's notice.

"I won't, but will it work on the canary?" I said.

She pursed her lips, considering. I could see the lie bubbling behind them.

"Come on, Marci," I said. "I have to get the bird back now. Will it work? Or is there something else I can try? I don't have much time."

Her round shoulders sagged. "It might. I don't know. To my knowledge no one has ever let the canary out of the cage before. But it's more dangerous than you can ever imagine."

"I know," I said solemnly. "Truly, I do. The magic keeps the dragons pinned and they have to stay that way. Believe me," I said, holding a hand over my heart, "the last thing I want to do is mess with those dragons."

A knowing look came into her eyes. "Had your fill of the roof?"

"Yes, ma'am," I said. "I sure did."

"Go give it a try. Whisper it. If it doesn't work, don't fool around with it, come straight back here," she said.

I bounded up. "I will." I scooted for the curtain. "You know who I saw when I put on that dress?"

She shook her head.

"You," I said, and skipped out of the room.

29

arvinder. The word throbbed on the tip of my tongue, three distinct syllables laced with enormous power. I threw open the closet door. I raced to the window and slapped my hand on the glass canary. At first, I didn't feel anything, and then the magic buzzed against my palm. I squeezed my eyes shut, concentrating. A fluttering sensation tickled my skin. The canary squirmed in the magic under my hand. His tiny heart beat with the pulse of the magic.

I parted my lips, ready to speak, but then, just beyond the canary I felt the gryphon brooding. His thoughts poured into me: soaring in the sky. I smelled the sharp scent of wind. The feathers in his mighty wings ruffled in flight. The sharp curve of his beak poised to speak. My fingers curled with the rending power in his talons. I felt myself tumbling toward him and yanked my hand from the glass.

Sarvinder buzzed in my mouth like an angry bee, cornered and ready to sting.

I gasped, dizzy and breathless. Releasing the canary was one thing; tampering with gryphons was quite another. I rubbed my palm against my apron, took a deep breath, and gingerly touched the glass canary. Splinters of rainbow dappled my apron as the sun's rays beat on the glass.

"Sarvinder," I whispered.

Sarvinder, the magic answered in a voice like a bell's chime.

Warmth balled up under my hand, rolling into a feathered, quivering mass. I pulled back and the canary *whoosh*ed out of the window and into the room. I gave him my finger and he latched on with his tiny talons. His tiny heart throbbed frantically. I wasted no time. I whipped the cage door open and thrust my hand, bird and all, inside. The canary hopped onto his little perch. I snatched my hand back and slapped the cage door shut. The lock clicked.

I exhaled in relief, pressing my forehead against the cage.

"It's all right now, Lyric, you're back safe and sound," I told him.

I blinked. I knew the canary's name! I realized I knew more than that.

"You're worried about the Princess," I told him, "because the magic is concerned about her. The magic *knows* her, even if she doesn't know it."

Lyric cocked his head at me, as if to say, *You've only now figured this out?*

"It's not like I had someone telling me this stuff," I told the bird. "You haven't helped much. I've had to figure it all out by myself."

Lyric whistled at me.

I decided to ignore that and picked up the cage.

"The Princess wants you back," I said. "I'm taking you to the dressing room."

Lyric banged his beak on the bars of his swing, but I held firmly to the cage's handle and turned to go. Behind me the dresses perked up, waving sleeves and ribbons, twirling laces.

I'd forgotten about them. I was glad they were back and not holding my misdeeds against me. A ruffle flared out at me, vying for my attention. I batted it aside.

"Hey, I'm glad to see you, ladies," I said. "But I have to leave—it's an emergency."

And then I beat it out of there before they could pressure me into giving in. The wardrobe hall was empty and so was the dressing room. I hung Lyric's cage on its stand. He shook out his wings and sang.

Lyric was happy. Princess Mariposa was happy when she came up to dress for dinner and found him serenading her. But I knew the dresses were not.

So that evening I snuck into the dressing room and borrowed the canary. Not that the Head Steward would have called it borrowing, but I did intend to put him back. Someone had to stop this wedding from happening.

Lyric sang the moment I took him into the closet, waking the dresses with a ripple of excitement. Skirts billowed. Sleeves flared.

"The Princess has called for the regalia; she means to marry Prince Baltazar, and he means to release the dragons," I cried to them.

Bodices swelled. Ribbons shook. Jewels gleamed in the dim closet like burning coals.

"Are you with me?"

The dresses strained at their hangers as if they would pull free and do battle for the Princess.

I set Lyric down on his table. I heard a *thump* behind me and turned to find hanger sixty-eight empty and a dusty-rose gown pooling on the carpet, its skirt flowing toward me.

"That one?" I asked Lyric, taking a step back from the overzealous dress.

He chirped his approval. I knelt down and picked it up. It was not the sort of dress I pictured heroines wearing as they rode into battle. Layers of dusty-rose chiffon gathered into a satin bodice with a bouquet of chiffon roses on the shoulders. But you didn't judge a dress by its fabric.

"Let's go get them," I told Sixty-Eight, and slipped it on.

It gripped me like a Laundress wringing out a shirt. I gasped, sucking in air. Then it snuggled into a perfect fit and did a jig around my knees with its many layers.

"Settle down," I said. "You can't draw attention to us or we'll be in serious trouble. Who'll save the Princess then?"

Sixty-Eight flounced once more and then lay quietly. In the mirror, a tall woman greeted me with a piercing stare. Streaks of pure white laced her dark hair. High cheek-bones, a long nose, and sharp blue eyes belied the bloom on her cheeks. Wearing a dark sapphire-blue dress with a high collar and a dazzling array of sapphires around her neck, she could have been Queen Candace herself. Or what I imagined Queen Candace to look like. I didn't know this imperious lady's name, but I'd seen her around the castle. Servants scurried out of her path. If anyone could follow Prince Baltazar without being questioned, it was her!

"I'll be back," I told Lyric, and set out.

I swept through the castle. Guards saluted me as I passed. Footmen bowed. I rounded a corner and there was Mrs. Pepperwhistle. My heart skipped a beat. She sank into a curtsy. I nodded at her and walked on. A trickle of sweat ran down my back. But she hadn't seen me—she'd seen Imperious Lady, whoever she was.

The rumble of conversation reached me from the mirrored hall. Something was happening in there. I strolled in, praying that Imperious Lady was nowhere in sight.

"Good evening, Baroness," said a man wearing a red coat.

"Good evening," I replied, glancing around the room. I was *Baroness* Imperious Lady.

The mirrored hall sparkled like a forest of glass. Great gold-framed mirrors reflected everything in the room, including the other mirrors, creating a kaleidoscope of colors and faces.

I caught sight of the Imperious Baroness and her piercing gaze in the mirror next to me. My heart froze. I turned around. The Baroness stared at me from every direction. It was only a reflection. I relaxed and began combing the room for Prince Baltazar.

People spoke to me, wishing me a good evening, calling me Lady Kaye, murmuring to their companions that *this* was the Baroness Azure. I nodded grandly at each one. My nods inspired warm smiles. Whoever this Baroness Lady Kaye Azure was, people wanted her approval.

Halfway down the room, I noticed an open door. I heard voices and peered in. Prince Baltazar, Princess

Mariposa, and Prince Sterling stood together over a large map spread out on a table.

"Good evening, Baroness," Princess Mariposa said. "We were admiring this new map, a wedding gift from Prince Sterling. Doesn't it have brilliant color?"

The map blazed in rich greens, blues, and reds, depicting a line of kingdoms, big and small, up and down the coastline. Eliora occupied the center, pinched between the White Sea and a range of mountains. Beyond the mountains sat the small kingdom of Tamzin. I wrinkled my nose; the name sounded familiar.

"Candala is a lovely shade of yellow," Prince Sterling said.

Prince Baltazar's lip curled at that, and he adjusted the map so that it faced away from Prince Sterling. Lemon-bright Candala lay far to the south, at the bottom of the map.

"Are you certain we shouldn't postpone the wedding until your family can arrive?" Princess Mariposa said, laying a hand on Prince Baltazar's sleeve.

He smiled at her with his weasel-like charm. "As an orphan, I have no family to send for."

"Oh," Princess Mariposa said.

"Tell me about Candala. What is it like?" Prince Sterling pressed.

"Paradise," Prince Baltazar replied. "Candala is known for its lakes."

My attention drifted back to Tamzin. *Tamzin.* Where had I seen that name before?

"It must be difficult to leave paradise for little Eliora," Prince Sterling replied, rolling up the map.

Prince Baltazar flushed to the roots of his wavy blond hair, branding Prince Sterling with a scorching look. He regained his composure with an effort, turning to the Princess and taking her hands in his.

"I intend to reside here, with you, my love," Prince Baltazar murmured, caressing the Princess's hands. "Compared with you, my kingdom means nothing to me."

Prince Sterling looked as disgusted as I felt. He slid the map into a leather tube and capped it. For a moment, he favored the Prince with a hard glance as if about to speak his mind. Then the Princess caught his eye, and his face softened into a warm smile.

"Your people will rejoice to see you crowned Queen at last," Prince Sterling told her.

"You should have crowned yourself Queen long ago," Prince Baltazar said.

The Princess blushed a deep scarlet. "My father's will," she replied, "dictated that I become Queen when I married."

"And you've honored your father's wishes," Prince Sterling agreed.

Prince Baltazar laughed. "I would think you could do whatever you wanted."

I thought of Prince Humphrey's butterfly and her father's wish that the two marry when they grew up.

"He just meant for you to be happy," I said, forgetting that I wasn't really a baroness.

"He did," Princess Mariposa said, surprised.

Prince Baltazar squeezed her waist. "I'll make you very happy, my love."

Prince Sterling buried his balled fist in his pocket. I hoped he'd slap the smirk off the Prince's laughing face, but he didn't. I wished I knew some clever questions a baroness could ask that would make Prince Baltazar reveal his true colors before it was too late. But nothing came to me.

"I'll have this map framed for Your Highness," Prince Sterling said.

As the Princess expressed her thanks, I glanced around, wondering where in the clutter of maps she would hang it, and saw a flash of white tail on a bookshelf.

I drifted about the room admiring the maps. At the bookshelf, I pulled a thick volume off a shelf and flipped it open, scanning the shelves for any sign of that white tail.

A tiny white head ducked out from behind a bookend

shaped like a porpoise. Two black eyes blinked at me. Iago! I nearly staggered with relief. He was all right.

"I'll talk to you upstairs," I whispered.

At this, he shook his head violently. He pointed to the bookshelf behind him.

I looked, but other than the porpoise, I couldn't see anything but old books.

Is it in a book? I mouthed, wondering what *it* might be.

He sighed. Then he put a paw to his heart and closed his eyes.

I waited until he opened them again, and then I guessed, "Are you afraid of the bookcase?"

This time, he shook so violently his whiskers had whiplash. He pointed up and to his heart and then he pointed at my wrist.

I shrugged, totally at a loss.

He sighed and vanished behind the porpoise. I waited as the heavy volume in my hands grew heavier, but he did not return. Finally, I put the book back and turned around to see what Prince Baltazar was up to now.

The room behind me was empty.

I had to keep tabs on the Prince. I had to find out who the Cloaked Lady was, and he was my only lead. I ducked my head out the door to look around the mirrored hall. And there right in front of me was an imperious silhouette in a sapphire-blue gown.

The Baroness stood two feet away, gesturing with a silver-capped cane. A knot of eager listeners surrounded her.

I ducked back into the map room. This was bad, very bad. I scrambled around the room for a place to hide and spotted a dark corner behind the bookcase. I sank down and melted into the wall.

I waited—and waited until every muscle ached and my knees turned to stone. I strained my ears for any sound, any hint that anyone was still in the hall, but heard only silence. At long last, I crept out and snuck a look around the doorway. The hall was empty; the lights were out. Only the reflected gleam of the mirrors played over the polished floor.

I'd missed my chance. The Princess had no doubt gone to bed long ago. And Prince Baltazar had gone too. Stewing with disappointment, I dragged Sixty-Eight back to the closet, put Lyric back in the dressing room, and crawled into bed, hoping that Iago would slip up onto my pillow and explain his cryptic messages. But if he did, I was already asleep.

30

The castle flooded with guests and every servant toiled from dawn until dark. Lindy volunteered me to press the monogrammed napkins for the feast. Each one had to be turned facedown and pressed into a thick towel to preserve the heavy raised embroideries in the corners. Lindy showed me the trick of it and then left me to slave away while she pressed acre after acre of tablecloths. Crate after crate of napkins arrived at my ironing board until my fingers cramped and my eyes crossed.

The servants soldiered on with grim expressions on their faces; the Princess's wedding would be the most magnificent ever. Or else. Every inch of the castle was scrubbed and polished, every goblet and plate shined, every bit of linen laundered, pressed, and hung up waiting for the day. The halls in the east wing resembled a massive sailor's ship, with flapping white cloths suspended from every wall.

I woke the morning of the wedding, stiff and sore.

"Everybody up," Francesca called.

A chorus of groans sounded around me. I pulled my covers over my head. A crackling sounded beneath me. I slid my hand under my pillow and felt a paper under there.

"That means you too, Darling," Francesca snapped, whipping my covers off my head.

I tucked my fist into my nightgown.

"I'm getting up," I groused.

Francesca turned away to pounce on the girl in the next bed. I tucked the paper under my blanket and dressed quickly, sitting back down on my bed to pull on my stockings and retrieve the paper, which I stashed in my pocket. Everyone else yawned, rubbing tousled heads and squinting blearily. I scooped up a roll and left them fishing for their clothes.

I paused in an empty corridor to read my note. Faint wavy lines traced out the letters *C-u-f-f.* Cuff? What did that mean? I turned the note over, looking for any hint of who had written it. A handful of printed words were on the other side. *Last over the wall,* the print said. Had it been torn out of a book? I eyed the edges, which had a nibbled appearance. Was this a message from Iago?

Could mice write? Well, could magical mice who jumped out of plaster friezes write? I had no idea. I stuffed the paper back in my pocket and headed off to work.

Princess Mariposa stood before the mirror in the dressing room, transformed into a beautiful bride in a lace dress. Lace gloves hid the Princess's hands. A long lace veil spilled from a diamond tiara set in her upswept ebony curls. Her changeable eyes turned a dark blue-green.

"Oh, goodness, Your Highness, if you don't beat all!" Lindy exclaimed.

"Truly lovely," Cherice agreed.

Lyric sang from his perch. I beamed at the Princess, too awed to speak.

A tall woman entered the room. Lady Kaye, Baroness Azure. She wore a green gown stiff with lace and embroidery and carried a cane I was pretty sure she didn't need. I gulped hard.

"I'm here to escort you, Mariposa," the Baroness said.

"Let's go down," the Princess agreed.

And they all left, Princess Mariposa on the Baroness's arm. Lindy and Cherice followed, reluctant to let the Princess out of their sight. I stood there, my hand in my pocket toying with my note. A weight settled on my heart.

It was over now. In a couple of hours the wedding would commence and Prince Baltazar would become the new owner of the King's regalia. The coronation of the two as King and Queen was scheduled for tomorrow. Prince Baltazar would be King Baltazar, ruler of Eliora and master of the dragons. I trembled at the thought.

Maybe I should grab Jane and make a run for it?

Coward, a voice in my head whispered to me.

My fists balled. My chin rose. I'd find the talisman myself and *borrow* it. Without the talisman, the dragons couldn't be freed. I'd hide it . . . somewhere. I didn't know where, but I'd think of some place. Some place outside the castle, maybe in the foothills beyond. It was a bold move, a dangerous move, but if I couldn't keep the Princess from marrying that weasel, I'd at least protect her from the dragons.

Or my name wasn't Darling Dimple!

"Lyric," I said, "let's get a dress!"

I snatched his cage off its hook and raced to Queen Candace's closet. The dresses gleamed in the bright morning light as I set the cage down on the table. A whisper went through them. I faced One Hundred, hands on my hips.

"I need a dress, a special dress, a dress that will allow me to go *anywhere*. Which dress would that be?" I asked.

One Hundred shook itself out and, lifting a lace sleeve,

pointed. I looked and saw Thirty-Three, a fawn-colored gown made of muslin and painted with bouquets of lilacs. A matching parasol hung from its hanger. It was the sort of ensemble that ladies wore on very warm afternoons. It looked like a frothy bit of fabric, but something about the way the bodice arched away from the hanger told me that this was one gown with steel in its seams.

"Do I need the parasol?" I asked the canary as I tugged on the dress. I pictured myself jabbing Prince Baltazar with its sharp metal point. "Should I take it in case I need a weapon?" I asked, settling Thirty-Three into place.

Lyric shook his head feathers.

"So no, I don't?"

He let out a sharp note.

I cast a longing look at its substantial ivory handle carved into the shape of an elephant. You could bash someone over the head with that. But then I'd have to keep track of it and I didn't want anything hindering my mission.

Lyric trilled at me impatiently.

"I'll leave it," I told him. "Don't nag."

My stomach did a flip-flop as I contemplated what I was about to do.

"I might not come back this time," I told Lyric and the dresses. "If I'm caught and captured, then, well, this is good-bye. So wish me luck." I saluted One Hundred, throwing back my shoulders and standing proudly. "For the Princess!" I cried, and whirled around to leave.

A tall woman, with a swanlike neck and a pile of luscious blond curls, wearing a brilliant pink, lace-trimmed gown, greeted me in the mirror. Cherice. I was Cherice! This was the perfect disguise. I'd grab the talisman and skip outside to hide it. Piece of cake!

Well, it would be a piece of cake once I figured out what the talisman was.

31

I slipped through the Princess's rooms with a shiver of anticipation. There was nothing in the bedroom, so I moved on to the sitting room. There, a series of gilt chests lay scattered around on the tables. The chests varied in size and decoration, but each had the royal crest mounted on top.

A long purple robe trimmed with ermine was draped over the sofa. I touched the robe; it was soft as snow. Gold-crusted epaulets rode on its shoulders and braided gold cords as thick as my fingers hung from both sides of the robe's opening. From the portrait of King Richard, I knew that the cords would be tied across the King's chest to keep the robe from falling off.

I surveyed the gilt chests. They held the greatest treasures of the kingdom, the King's regalia. Each piece was worn for the coronation of a new king. The idea that I, Darling Dimple, Under-presser, would open these chests and gaze upon these treasures left me temporarily numb.

Thirty-Three quivered against me.

"I can't just stand by and let those dragons be loosed. I have to do something," I told it.

But the hollow in my stomach warned me that touching these treasures was a worse crime than any I'd ever thought of. These weren't merely the possessions of Princess Mariposa's grandfather, King Richard; these emblems of royal authority went back into the mists of time. Kings of Eliora had worn these as long as there had been a kingdom. Except for one piece, that is, the talisman. That had been made for Richard.

It occurred to me that if the dragons hadn't burned down the old castle back then, there would have been portraits of all those old kings. I could have skipped from picture to picture, comparing, until I discovered which piece was different. All these treasures must have been lugged out of the burning castle for safekeeping. I wondered if they still smelled like smoke.

I leaned over the robe and sniffed. The smell of mothballs assailed my nose. And something else—spirits of orange. The Princess had ordered all of it cleaned and polished; smells wouldn't help me. I would have to start digging through them all.

I opened the biggest chest first. A puff of incense rose out of the satin lining, making my nose burn. Evidently, these didn't get opened very often. They could probably use a good airing. On a bed of satin sat the great crown of Eliora, a gold-covered, diamond-blazing, emerald-studded monster. It looked so heavy that I imagined my neck snapping under the weight. I decided that it couldn't be the talisman and closed the lid.

The next chest was long and narrow; it held a sword that rested in a jeweled scabbard. I touched it, testing for the presence of magic. I assumed the talisman would buzz under my touch like the stained-glass canary did. I didn't feel anything. The next long chest held the scepter, a silver staff topped with a diamond the size of a goose egg. I slipped my hand under it and lifted it an inch off the satin lining. It balanced cold and heavy on my palm. I put it down. It seemed to me that the talisman would be smaller, something easy to hold or wield.

A sash woven from cloth of gold and embroidered with pearls lay in the next chest. Another held a ring, a ruby-eyed gold lion's head. I slid it on my finger. The lion's head swung around my thin finger and hung below my hand. I straightened it up and held it in place with my other hand. Then I closed my eyes and felt for the castle's magic.

Silence hummed in my ears. Thirty-Three jiggled impatiently on my hips. I opened my eyes and put the ring back in its box. I was a little sorry; a ring would have been the easiest thing to tuck in a pocket and sneak out of the castle.

A chest with a ruby-tipped handle held the chain of office. A thick gold many-pointed medallion swung between double rows of thick gold links. A starburst was emblazoned on the center of the medallion. A diamond sat in the center of the starburst. I traced the starburst etching and felt the smallest *sizzle* of power. Could this be it? I bent over it and whispered in a voice so faint that it was barely a breath: *Sarvinder.* Nothing. The metal turned to ice beneath my finger. I rocked back on my heels. This was not it. I could have sworn it was! It had the same starburst that was on the terrace where Princess Mariposa showed me the dragons.

Swallowing the bitter taste of disappointment, I turned to the remaining chests. They held a series of smaller objects: several sets of buttons—diamond, amethyst, and onyx, all set in gold. I supposed they were sewn on whatever waistcoat the King wore for special occasions and then cut off for another use. A belt buckle worked with two gryphons facing each other. A grouping of small carved stones set on clips. They looked a little like the trim on some of the Princess's slippers, so I assumed they were meant to be worn on the King's shoes. A pair of silver spurs. I was excited by another, smaller ring of a lizard swallowing its tail. Holding my breath, I slipped it on.

Nothing.

The last chest held a set of heavy gold bracelets about two inches wide; each had an odd pointed design on the top. I picked one up. Inside the bracelet ruby letters glowed, spelling out V-I-N-D-E-R. I picked up the other. Inside it were the letters S-A-R. I set the two bracelets together; they fitted perfectly. The odd design on the surface formed a starburst. SARVINDER burned on the inside with a ruby-tinged fire.

Cuffs! This was what Iago had meant. These cuffs were the talisman.

Did Princess Mariposa know?

I swayed, suddenly dizzy with fear. I had in my hands the powerful talisman that controlled the golden collars of the ferocious dragons chained to the roof! My tongue clung to the roof of my mouth. Black spots swam before my eyes.

I dropped the cuffs back into their chest. They sank into their bed of satin with an audible *hiss*. I wiped my damp palms on Thirty-Three. I'd found them. Now what did I do? I couldn't skip out of the castle toting a chest under my arm, even as Cherice. The chest was bound to raise eyebrows, if not summon Guards. And the cuffs alone were big and heavy, much too heavy to slip on my skinny wrists and wear. And much too bulky to pop in my pocket and sashay down the hall. I would list to one side. That would not be good. Not to mention the huge bulge in my pocket that even Thirty-Three might not cover up.

There had to be a way to sneak them out without calling attention to myself. What could I put them in that Cherice had been seen carrying? I'd seen Lindy with her picnic basket under her cloak. I'd never seen Cherice with anything other than her magnifying glass.

I needed something close at hand. A laundry basket would be too big. Cherice had a sewing box, but she kept it locked in her desk. Why, I had no idea. Scissors, spools of thread, and a packet of needles—why lock those up? Not that it mattered, because she had her keys with her. I couldn't get into her desk without breaking a lock. That would raise questions.

So would the missing cuffs, and who would be the first person they looked for? Me, that's who, because everyone else was downstairs preparing for the wedding. I not only needed a plan for getting the cuffs out of the castle, I needed an alibi. I wiped my brow. This was not going to be a piece of cake.

I heard muffled voices coming from the Princess's bedroom. I shut the chest.

"They are laid out in there," a woman's voice said.

They were coming my way. Dress or no dress, it would not be easy to explain what I was doing in here to one of the Princess's ladies. Especially not one who'd seen Cherice somewhere else. I whipped around, hunting for a place to hide. Spindly chairs didn't offer much cover. I had to get out.

I heard the knob on the door to the bedroom turn.

I dived through the only other door available—the door to the butterfly room. The white butterflies bobbed on their silver cords overhead. To anyone looking in, disguised in Cherice's brilliant pink, I stood out like a flamingo in the all-white room.

"We haven't much time," Prince Baltazar said from behind the not-quite-closed door. "I can't miss my own wedding." He chuckled.

I balled my fists. I glanced around the room full of cabinets and display cases. There was nowhere to go, and I wanted to hear more of what was said. A narrow table stood against the wall by the door. It wasn't much cover, but anyone glancing in probably wouldn't look under the table. I ducked beneath it, tucked Thirty-Three close to me, and scooted back until my spine met the wall. I pressed my ear to the door.

I heard the opening and slamming of chests.

"Aha! Here we go," a woman's voice proclaimed. I'd heard that voice before; it was the Cloaked Lady's, the kind of voice that didn't have to be loud to be heard, a voice that commanded attention.

I twisted Thirty-Three's skirt in my hands. The Cloaked Lady was only a few feet away. I wondered if there was any way I could sneak a peek at her.

"Are you sure this is it?" Prince Baltazar spoke.

"The magnifying glass does not lie!" the woman snapped.

"Sure. Whatever you say. So how do they work?" Prince Baltazar asked in a soothing tone.

"You put them together—see where the design meets—and they form a starburst."

A starburst. Dread washed over me. Prince Baltazar and the Cloaked Lady had found the talisman so fast it made my head spin. Any minute now they were going to use it!

"They don't work," Prince Baltazar complained.

"You have to wear them and then bring them together; there is little use in holding them," she scolded.

"They're stiff. Ouch! It bit my wrist!"

"Fool, it's a piece of metal; turn them sideways and slide them on!"

"They're warm," Prince Baltazar gasped.

"Use them! Use them now!"

I heard a faint ringing as the two cuffs met. I tensed up,

squeezing Thirty-Three in my sweaty hands, and waited for the roof to explode.

Nothing happened.

"Is this all?" Baltazar said. "There's nothing. *Nothing.* What else do I do?"

The castle wall behind me pulsed. I felt the magic in it awaken and surge into my spine. My every hair stood on end. My every nerve tingled.

"Perhaps you must concentrate. Say a command," the Cloaked Lady said.

A louder ring sounded as the two cuffs clanged together.

"Dragons, be free!" Prince Baltazar shouted.

Nothing.

"Hush," she said. "Not so loud."

"Collars, release!" he said as if through gritted teeth. "I command you to work!"

Then I knew it as surely as the magic buzzing in the wall and in my spine: the cuffs worked with the magic word. Had they not seen the letters inside the cuffs?

"*Sarvinder,*" I breathed.

As the word left my lips, the air around me tingled. The wall throbbed. I clapped my hand over my mouth. Oh, no! Had I helped release the dragons? I heard a tinkling sound like the breaking of glass and then the flutter of wings. Looking out from under the table, I saw scores of real butterflies where the white ones had hung. A storm of wings blew around the room in a colorful flurry. They lit on cabinets and tables and walls.

They flew under the table, surrounding me, settling on my hair and shoulders and knees. Their wings beat in rhythm. I sat as still as possible, coated in glorious, beautiful butterflies! I'd released the butterflies on the ceiling. All of them. They must have been held captive like the mice in the frieze.

If only the Princess were here to see her long-lost butterflies.

"They don't work!" Prince Baltazar said. I heard the clank of metal being tossed down.

"Are you sure? I thought I heard something," the Cloaked Lady said.

"Did you hear the sound of dragons screaming through the air?" Prince Baltazar asked with a snarl. "It didn't work."

"Maybe we're too far away; maybe we have to be on the roof."

Maybe you had to have the magic word.

"Well, there isn't time now," he snapped. "Pick those up and put them back. I'll have plenty of time to play with them after the wedding."

"The talisman was the goal, not the wedding," the woman argued. "Let's take them."

Butterflies coated my cheeks and kissed my eyelids. I waved them away, flailing blindly. My hand met a table leg with a *thunk*. I froze, hand outstretched, butterflies nibbling my ears.

"Someone's in there," the woman said, pushing open the door and walking into the room.

Her brilliant pink skirt brushed my feet. My heart sputtered in my chest. Thirty-Three crackled in fear. I was in terrible, terrible trouble.

"Wretched creatures! The place is full of them," she said, swatting the air.

A butterfly fell to the floor. I swallowed, watching it flutter brokenly against the tile.

"Well, well, what have we here?" the woman said. She bent down.

Blinking butterflies out of my way, I found myself staring into the face of Cherice.

32

Cherice's eyes flew open. Her chin dropped. Her face paled.

"Who are you?" she gasped.

"I—I—I," I said.

Her eyes trailed up and down my huddled form. She gaped at me as if she saw a ghost. Her hand flew to the lace at her neckline as if she was reassuring herself that she still wore her dress. She didn't see me, Darling Dimple. She saw herself.

I swallowed, pulling Thirty-Three tighter to my knees. If I didn't tell her who I was, she wouldn't know. She reached under the table, grabbed the front of Thirty-Three, and hauled me out.

"Who are you?" she demanded, shaking me.

"Cherice," I said.

"Imposter!" she roared. "Tell me your name!"

She hauled me up so that my feet dangled an inch off the ground. I felt the seams in Thirty-Three brace themselves. If the dress tore, it was all over.

"Who is it?" Prince Baltazar said from the doorway. He was dressed in a splendid silver coat with diamond buttons. His wavy hair was slicked down and the overpowering odor of cologne steamed out of his ruffled shirt front. Several butterflies found this smell alluring and clung to his sleeve.

Cherice dropped me and spun me around. My eyeballs rolled around in their sockets.

"Look!" she croaked. This Cherice didn't speak in the warm sugary voice I was used to. This Cherice sounded like the Cloaked Lady.

Prince Baltazar flinched at the sight of me.

"Who are you?" he demanded.

"Isn't it obvious?" Cherice snapped. "She's a spy! Look, she's even dressed like me. That dressmaker must be in on it." A butterfly settled on her hair; she batted it away.

"In on what?" he asked, staring at me as if I couldn't really be there.

"Who else is in this with you?" she asked, shaking me. "Who else wants the talisman?"

I pressed my lips together and shook my head. I wasn't going to say anything.

"I'll make you talk," she told me, pinching my arm.

"There isn't time; the wedding begins in another hour," Prince Baltazar said, snapping out of his daze. "Let's do something with her for now and deal with this later."

"Bother the wedding; grab the cuffs and let's get away," Cherice snarled. "The imposter can have a little accident."

She sprinted to a window and flung it open. The butterflies, sensing freedom, flowed out into the breeze. I squeaked like a mouse stuck with a pin.

Prince Baltazar grabbed my upper arm. "No."

I went limp with relief. I didn't like to think about how far down to the ground it was.

Cherice turned around, cheeks as pink as her dress. "What do you mean, no?"

The Prince dusted butterflies off his sleeve with his free hand and patted his hair. "We don't want the commotion. I can't miss my wedding. Once I am married to the Princess, there will be plenty of time for other things."

"You double-crossing idiot!" she growled. "I'll expose you!"

He smiled his oiliest smile. He was more evil than I'd even imagined. I eyed the half-open door. There was no way I could get away, not while he had an iron grip on me. I braced myself to scream.

"Until now, we've done it your way. Now, we'll do it my way. My pet, don't you see? Once I am King, then anything is possible," Prince Baltazar said.

"Once *you* are King? Don't delude yourself. Mariposa will never let you loose those dragons," she said in a steely voice, coming right up to him and staring in his face. "And what about me?"

"You," he said, patting her cheek and pulling me close enough in the process to get a nose-burning whiff of his cologne. "You can console me when poor little Mariposa gets eaten by a dragon."

The air left my lungs as if someone had punched me in the middle. This couldn't be happening.

"Killing Mariposa was never part of the plan," Cherice said.

"Who needs a busybody around? Once she's gone, you'd be the new Queen." He lowered his voice. "You'd like that, wouldn't you, love? Queen Cherice. Has a nice ring to it."

"These people follow Mariposa because she's their Princess; they won't follow you just because you wear a crown," Cherice said.

"They'll have to, once the dragons are my attack dogs," he said with a smirk. "And besides, love, you'd better stop and think. If I fall, you fall. If I succeed, you succeed. There's no going back now."

Cherice eyed him and licked her lower lip in a very unladylike manner.

"What about her?" she asked, nodding at me.

I looked back and forth at the hard expressions on the two of them. My knees went weak. I opened my mouth to scream, but the Prince slapped his hand over it.

"Her friends will always wonder what became of her," Prince Baltazar said, pulling a sad face. "Where can we stash her until later?"

Cherice looked around. "Not in Mariposa's rooms."

"Somewhere close," he suggested.

She snapped her fingers. "Lindy's closet. No one will look there."

"Not even Lindy?" he asked.

"She'll be chasing after that addlepated Captain of hers," Cherice answered with a smug grin. "Get her and come with me."

He picked me up and held me kicking and squirming against his chest.

"Lead on," he said.

Cherice walked back into the sitting room and Prince Baltazar followed, clutching me close. The chest for the cuffs was still open and Cherice stopped to close it.

"Wait. Put them on me. I want to see what they might do outside and I don't want to come back up here," he said.

A suspicious gleam lit Cherice's eyes, but she did as he said. She put the cuffs on him, hiding them under his sleeves. Then she motioned for silence and walked to the bedroom door. She opened it an inch and looked out.

Then she walked through. Prince Baltazar dogged her steps. I fought as hard as I could, but his arms were like steel bands around me.

I was trapped. If only a Footman or a lady or even Francesca would show up and stop them. But no, every room was deserted. They kept up the same caution at every door until we reached the pressing room. And there they shoved me in Lindy's cupboard. I stumbled in, gasping for breath, and fell headfirst into Lindy's long black cloak.

Behind me, the cupboard door slammed shut and the lock clicked.

I heard the sound of their footsteps as they went away. I sobbed into Lindy's cloak. I had really and truly failed this time. It was all over. My shoulders shook with my sobs. Princess Mariposa would marry that monster and then later, when everyone was feasting, Cherice would come back for me.

I shuddered to think what she'd do to me. Kill me—that was what she'd do. I looked around in the pitch-blackness. There was no way out. Bile rose up in my throat. I choked, sick with fear. I clutched the cloak. Would I ever be found? Would anyone miss me? Thirty-Three squeezed me.

Oh, no. I gasped. Would I still look like Cherice when I was dead?

"I'm sorry, I'm so sorry," I told Thirty-Three. "You'll die too. I got you into this and now you're stuck."

Thirty-Three squeezed me again. I sank to my knees, hugging myself into a tight little ball, and crying afresh. Jane! She'd never know what happened to me. She'd think I ran away. She'd be brokenhearted.

A huge sob strangled me. I wanted Jane so bad I couldn't stand it. I didn't want any stupid old adventure. I wanted to run back to the under-cellar and have my old friends back. I'd scrub pots with vigor and never have another adventure as long I lived.

Thirty-Three pinched my shoulders with a bite as sharp as a snake's. I jumped, raising my head and blinking through swollen eyes.

"Hey, stop," I bawled. "I said I was sorry. You don't have to be mean. I'll be just as dead as you."

The skirt of Thirty-Three rolled up and slapped me in the face.

Stunned, I stopped bawling.

A furry tickling sensation touched my hand. Tiny paws gripped my sleeve and raced up my arm.

"Iago?" I cried. "Is that you?"

He nuzzled my chin, tickling me with his tail. I reached up to stroke his furry back. He squirmed; he felt warm and alive under my hand. I wasn't alone in the dark after all.

"Did the magic send you? How did you get in here? Is there a hole somewhere?"

I thought about feeling around to find it and then decided that it didn't matter. He was here. I wasn't alone. Then I realized that if he had been able to get in, he must be able to get back out.

"Oh, Iago, can you get me out? Can you unlock the cupboard?"

He tapped my chin with his tail. I strained my eyes, sucking in a breath of dusty, spirits-of-orange-scented air. It was too dark to see him, too dark for him to act out his answers. I really, *really* wished I spoke Mouse. He tapped my chin again. He was trying to tell me something.

"Tell me yes or no. One tap for yes. Two taps for no," I said, eager to understand.

He tapped me once.

"Can you open the door?"

No.

"Can you get back out?"

Yes.

If he could get out, then he could go for help!

Jane?

Jane was blind as a bat. She'd never see Iago or his pantomimes. And even if she felt him, she wouldn't know that he was anything but an ordinary mouse. She'd probably go after him with a broom. And I'd still be locked in the cupboard. The wedding would still take place. Prince Baltazar would still be King. I needed someone else.

"Can you find Gillian? Can you get Roger?" I wailed.

Yes.

He slid down my arm and vanished into the darkness of the closet.

I dried my eyes on Lindy's cloak. Iago would get help. Any minute now, Gillian and Roger would burst into the room to save me. Well, they would if they weren't still too mad at me to come.

33

I couldn't see anything in the total darkness of the cupboard. Perspiration covered my face. It was dark and hot. My chest constricted. I reached out to feel that the walls were still where they belonged and not creeping closer, not squishing me in a wooden vise. I wondered how long I'd been in there. An hour? Two?

I strained my ears, listening for the sound of Cherice's quick, light steps. I groped around the cupboard, feeling for a weapon. My fingers closed on the broom. I grasped the handle and stood up, feeling around until I was sure I was facing the door. I'd hear her coming and when she unlocked the door, I'd whack her as hard as I could.

I wouldn't give up without a fight.

Thud. Thud. Thud. Someone was coming, and it didn't

sound like Cherice. Fear gripped me by the throat. I clutched my broom, ready to spring. If it was Prince Balta-zar, I'd aim for his stomach. I'd only get one chance, so I had to jab as hard as I could.

"Darling? Are you in here?" a voice said.

It was a voice I wasn't certain I'd hear again, and it sounded like music.

"Roger!" I called. "Is that you, Roger?"

"Where are you?" he said, walking around.

"Here! I'm in here," I yelled. I dropped the broom and pounded on the door with both fists. "Let me out!"

The door opened so suddenly that I fell forward, blinded by the bright light. I hit something solid, and it and I crashed to the floor in a heap. Stars revolved inside my head as I groped for something solid to hang on to. I caught an arm and latched on.

It was a wiry, strong arm in a rough shirtsleeve. It felt wonderful. It smelled a little like manure. It smelled heav-enly. I squinted; Roger's freckled face swam into view. I was so glad to see him that I almost kissed him. Then I saw the mouse clinging to his collar.

"Iago! You got help!" I cried. "Thank you."

Roger sat back; a look of horror marred his freckles. His cap had fallen off and his hair stood straight up. "I'm sorry, lady," he sputtered. "I thought you were someone else."

"No, it's me," I said, breathing in the fresh-linen smell of the pressing room. I giggled, deliriously happy to be out of the cupboard.

"O . . . kay," he said slowly. He dug a note out of his pocket and handed it to me. I took the jagged-edged triangle of print-covered paper and turned it over. Coarse writing on it read *Darling in danger.*

"Iago, you wrote him a note!" I frowned, puzzled. "Where's Gillian?"

"Gillian?" Roger said. "She went outside to sneak a peek at the wedding."

"Oh." Of course she did. Every girl in the castle wanted to see it.

"Well, okay, lady, I have to get back to work," Roger said.

"What?" I clutched my dress, remembering. "It's me, Darling. Really. I can prove it. Come with me."

I jumped up. Roger grabbed his cap and got up slowly, keeping his eye on me the whole time. He set his cap on his head. Iago climbed up onto his shoulder. I held out my hand.

"Come on," I said.

He stuck his hands in his pants pockets. *Boys.* I snorted.

"Follow me," I ordered.

I raced to Queen Candace's closet; Roger followed me

in, dragging his feet. Lyric ruffled his feathers when Roger walked into the room. I slithered out of Thirty-Three and put it back on its hanger. He saw and stopped in his tracks.

"Darling?" Roger gasped.

"I told you it was me," I said. "The dress is a disguise."

Roger yanked off his cap and scratched his head, the picture of confusion.

"What? How? Where'd you get it?"

A burst of trumpets broke through the silence in the closet. I ran to the window and cranked it open. Outside, far below on the western lawns, I spied the waving pennants of the gaily striped tents set up for the feast. I craned forward, bracing myself on the stone gryphon for a better look.

The terraces below me were decorated in flowered arches. The wedding was set to be held on the terrace with the starburst, followed by a feast on the lawn. Later, a ball would be held in the ballroom, followed by fireworks. Brightly dressed people the size of ants scurried about the terrace. Underneath me, a tiny figure in white appeared.

Princess Mariposa! She was on her way to her wedding. It wasn't too late!

Lyric whistled at me.

I turned to him. "I know!" I cried. "What do I do?"

It was a long, long way through the castle to the western terrace. Even if I got there in time, Guards were sure to stop me. Prince Baltazar would marry her and be our new King. I leaned out the window, biting my lip, broiling with anxiety.

"What do you do about what?" Roger asked, coming up behind me.

"I have to stop the wedding!" I said.

Under my hands, I felt a tingle of waking magic in the stone gryphon's head. Through the granite the feathered head of the gryphon shifted. I felt its strength. I felt its thoughts, flying, hunting, screaming. And then I felt something else: amusement.

"What is so funny?" I asked it.

You, the stone gryphon murmured to me through the magic. *Unable to fly down and save her.*

"This whole thing is funny," Roger replied.

"Can you stop Baltazar? Can you?"

The gryphon chuckled. *Release me and I will.*

"Stop who? You're going to get in real trouble, Darling," Roger warned.

I had a sudden memory of the sharp beak and rending claws of the hunting gryphon.

"Not to kill him," I whispered, warning it. "Just to stop him."

Release me.

275

A silver speck joined the Princess. There was no time to do anything else. I closed my eyes, hoping that I was doing the right thing, and reached for the magic.

"Darling, get back in here, you'll fall. We can sneak downstairs and watch if you want to see the wedding that bad."

"*Sarvinder,*" I whispered.

The stone shattered as the gryphon broke free from the castle. It spread its massive wings, shook its feathered head, flexed its terrible claws, and lashed at the castle with its lionlike tail. With a bloodcurdling shriek, it shot into the air and soared up to block the sun. Then it dived like a hawk, straight for the terrace below.

I fell back inside, shaking. Lyric gripped his perch, blinking rapidly.

"I had to," I said. "There's no time."

Roger stood, openmouthed. I almost felt sorry for him; he looked so scared. But I didn't have any more time. I had a wedding to break up.

"Come on, Roger," I cried. "We have to stop that wedding!"

Then I grabbed hold of him and dragged him along with me.

३४

Pandemonium reigned on the terrace when we arrived. The gryphon had landed on the starburst, scattering fancy white chairs and toppling arches. Flowers and broken crockery littered the paving stones that glittered in the sunlight. The powerful haunches of the gryphon tensed and relaxed. Its long, fur-tipped tail swayed back and forth like a serpent. Its massive wings beat the air. A group of Guards confronted the beast, swords pointed at its chest.

Captain Bryce stood with his sword outstretched and his other arm behind him, urging Princess Mariposa to stay back. A group of Archers ran up the terrace steps. Wedding guests huddled in groups, hiding behind the Princess.

Princess Mariposa had thrown down her bouquet and

hitched up her long train. She faced the gryphon, trembling but regal, unwilling to run away or back down.

"Let him go!" she commanded.

Roger and I inched closer to the terrace. I gripped his sweaty hand in mine. Prince Baltazar sprawled on the pavement, pinned down by the gryphon's powerful talons. He lay on his back, white-faced and wide-eyed, too terrified to speak. His splendid silver coat fell from his shoulders in tatters. A diamond button had rolled across the pavement and sparkled in the sun like a tiny fire. The gryphon puffed out its chest, arched its neck, and screamed. Prince Baltazar fainted.

I clapped my hands over my ears. The Guards quaked in terror but stood their ground. Wedding guests called out for the Guards to save them. I felt, deep down, the amused chuckle of the gryphon, which irked me. If I were one of those Guards facing an enormous half-eagle, half-lion monster, I'd be frightened too.

Monster? the gryphon huffed.

I stared at the gryphon. I could *hear* it in my head. Without touching the castle. A tingling from the magic lingered in my fingers, my hair, and the very air around me.

The Archers fell to one knee and nocked their arrows, sighting the feathered chest.

"Stop!" I yelled, and broke free from Roger. Then I

jumped in front of the gryphon, waving my arms in the air. "Don't shoot."

"Darling, no!" Princess Mariposa cried.

"Darling," Captain Bryce called, "get out of there!"

"Darling, are you crazy?" Roger roared.

The scent of crushed flowers and the raw-earth smell of spilled potting soil hovered in the warm air. The sun blazed. I glanced down. Prince Baltazar bled from a cut on his forehead. The paving stone beside him bore scratches from the gryphon's talons.

An unbroken urn slammed over and Gillian bounded up over it, sailing through the air, armed with a fork. She landed before the gryphon and brandished her fork.

"Leave her alone, you beast," she cried, curls flying, eyes flashing.

A fork? It was sure brave of her—stupid, but brave. I grabbed her arm.

"Wait," I said. "It's okay, Gillian, stand back."

Gripping her fork, she backed away, keeping an eye on the gryphon. Roger snatched her by the apron tie and yanked her back to where he stood.

I turned to face the Princess. What could I say next? I could tell them that the Prince was a liar and a schemer. But what proof did I have? I'd told the gryphon to stop him and it had, but I had no guarantee that the massive beast behind me would obey any more of my orders. Sweat trickled down my back.

"Darling," Princess Mariposa called, shoving past the Captain, "come here right now."

It's a dilemma, the gryphon agreed.

"He's a thief," I cried as loud as I could.

Really? the gryphon said.

"Darling," Princess Mariposa warned.

"He took part of the regalia," I told her, pointing to his wrists. "He stole the cuffs out of your room. He's wearing them right now."

She blinked, uncertain.

I knelt down and yanked back his sleeve. The bright gold of the cuff gleamed in the sunlight.

"He took them. That's what I ran down here to tell you," I said.

The whole crowd gasped.

In the distance, the sound of marching boots rang out. The Captain looked over his shoulder, perplexed. Sweat ran down my face and burned in my eyes. I wiped it away with my sleeve. The gryphon stirred behind me. Prince Baltazar hadn't moved. I hoped that didn't mean he was dead, but I didn't look to see. Because just then, a troop of men marched down the walkway carrying two standards, one red and the other green. Neither was the silver-gray of Eliora.

This is getting interesting, the gryphon mused.

Gillian dropped her fork.

The troop parted the dazed wedding guests like a comb through wet hair. Two men marched at the head of the troop: a tall, silver-haired man in a red cloak and Prince Sterling. I blinked. Prince Sterling no longer looked impoverished. Now he wore clothes befitting a king and bore a jeweled sword at his side.

"Halt and identify yourselves," Captain Bryce called out.

The men halted before the gryphon and saluted the Princess in unison.

You should join your Princess, the gryphon said, reaching down and nudging me with the broad side of its curved beak.

I stumbled forward. The feel of that hard beak against my back convinced me. I ran to Princess Mariposa's side just as the man in the red cloak knelt before Her Highness.

"I come in friendship," the man said in a loud voice.

"Rise in friendship," Princess Mariposa said, stepping forth. "And name yourself."

The man rose. He was as tall and powerfully built as Prince Baltazar and as handsome, despite the fact that he was much older. He bowed.

"I am Baltazar, Prince of Candala, Your Grace," he said, his voice ringing across the terrace.

The terrace erupted in a roar of outrage. Princess Mariposa paled. Captain Bryce lowered his sword. I stuffed my fist in my mouth. Princess Mariposa reached for me, drawing me to her side as if to protect me.

The Prince held up his hand and the crowd quieted.

"I apologize for disrupting your day and ruining your wedding," the real Prince Baltazar said with the trace of a smile. "But I couldn't let you marry an imposter."

"Where's your proof?" Captain Bryce asked, eyeing the men who accompanied the new prince.

The real Prince held out his hand. "I wear the ring, the great seal of the kingdom of Candala. Does your man bear such an emblem?"

Princess Mariposa stepped forward and took the Prince's hand in hers. She studied the heavy gold ring. And then she gazed up at Prince Sterling.

"I can vouch for the Prince of Candala," he said. "I have a letter from King Lawrence of Tamzin as well." He reached inside his coat, pulled out a folded parchment bearing a heavy seal, and handed it to her.

She took the letter and broke the seal. Everyone waited with bated breath as she read its contents. Tears welled up in her eyes. She folded the letter.

"I see," Princess Mariposa said in a hushed voice.

At this, the gryphon reared up, holding the fake Baltazar up in its claw and dangling him in the air. The fake

Baltazar woke with a scream and cried out for help. His nose bled, marring the starched ruffles of his once-white shirt.

Who is this? the gryphon wondered, cocking his head at me.

"Who is that?" Princess Mariposa asked, pointing at the fake Baltazar.

A wave of butterflies drifted down over the scene like brightly colored confetti. One landed on the gryphon's crest. Another settled on the real Prince Baltazar's head.

"Dudley, a former gardener of mine, I'm afraid. I turned him out for stealing," the real Prince Baltazar said.

The fake Prince erupted in a torrent of curses.

"You turned him out?" Princess Mariposa said to the real Prince.

"His mother begged for mercy and the goods had been recovered. . . ." The Prince trailed off, shrugging his shoulders. "I had no idea he'd cause Your Highness such grief."

Tears streamed down the Princess's face; she dabbed at them with her veil.

"Why?" she asked. "Why?"

One of the Princess's tears splashed on the top of my head. I fought the urge to cry too. I'd wanted to stop the wedding, but I hadn't wanted her to be sad. I had to do something, say something. I tugged on her lace sleeve.

She peered down at me. I motioned for her to come

closer. She bent over and I whispered in her ear, "He was looking for the talisman."

Princess Mariposa looked me in the eye. I met her gaze squarely. Her tears vanished. She set her jaw like steel. Then she straightened up.

"Remove the King's cuffs from that imposter!" she commanded.

Captain Bryce squared his shoulders and stalked over to the dangling imposter. Dudley—it was hard to think of him as Dudley after knowing him so long as Prince Baltazar—kicked at the Captain, snarling. The gryphon dumped Dudley on the pavement at the Captain's feet with a bone-cracking *snap*. The Captain knelt down and wrenched the cuffs off the hapless Dudley.

The gryphon snagged Dudley's coattail with the tip of a talon.

Let me have him, the gryphon said, its eyes boring into mine.

"The gryphon wants him," I told the Princess, whose eyes grew wide.

"To—to kill him?" she gasped.

To take him away. Far away, the gryphon replied, its tongue curling in its open beak.

I had the feeling it wasn't telling me the whole truth.

"It says it wants to take him far away," I said.

Prince Baltazar shrugged. "There is a certain justice to that request. He's caused a lot of trouble and, I think"—the Prince looked down at Princess Mariposa in compassion—"a lot of heartbreak."

Tell her I promise to never return to her kingdom, the gryphon offered.

"The gryphon promises to never come back," I added. "It's a good trade. Gryphons are powerful hunters, and now that this one is loose . . ." I looked up at the damaged turret where the beast had once been stone.

"They're lies! Lies!" Dudley screamed. "Ask my wife; she'll tell you!"

"Wife?" Princess Mariposa roared.

I blinked. Of course, that explained a great deal.

"Cherice," I told her. She glared down at me. I shrank— suddenly aware that I should be quiet and mind my own business.

"Guards!" Princess Mariposa's voice rang out like the sound of a sword drawn from a scabbard. "Find the Wardrobe Mistress and detain her."

Guards scrambled to beat each other back into the castle.

"Sir Gryphon, I accept your word to leave my kingdom and never return. But mark me, sir, I show no mercy to those who break their vows," Princess Mariposa said.

"Mariposa! No! Wait!" Dudley wailed as the gryphon rolled him up in its talons and, with a slap of its great wings, soared up into the sky.

And with it, I felt the last wisp of magic drip out of my fingers. I swayed, slightly dizzy.

Princess Mariposa turned away. Captain Bryce gripped the gold cuffs. The Archers lowered their arrows. Wedding guests crept out from behind the shattered remains of the royal wedding. The real Prince Baltazar tugged at his collar. Prince Sterling looked at his boots.

A tall figure in a stiff green gown banged the pavement with her cane.

"No doubt your cooks have prepared a grand feast," Lady Kaye said.

She patted the Princess's hand.

"My dear, let me escort your guests to their refreshments," Lady Kaye said. Then she lowered her voice and spoke close to the Princess's ear. "I think you'd like some time alone."

Princess Mariposa nodded.

The Baroness Azure raised her regal head and proclaimed, "The Princess requests your presence at her feast, which will now be held in the royal dining room. Please follow me." Holding her cane aloft, the Baroness marched back to the castle, stepping over debris as if it weren't there.

The shocked guests ambled after her, some glancing back at the Princess, who stood proud and pale at Prince Baltazar's side.

"I hope you can forgive me," Prince Baltazar began.

Princess Mariposa laid a hand on his arm. "You've traveled a great distance to spare me from a shocking disgrace. Please stay as my guest and attend my feast."

The Prince grinned. "I am a little hungry," he said with a glance at Prince Sterling. "Care to join me, Humphrey?"

"Humphrey?" Princess Mariposa gasped, turning pale for a second time that morning.

"My pardon, this is my friend, Prince Humphrey of Tamzin," Prince Baltazar explained.

"Humphrey Frederic Albert Sterling," Prince Sterling corrected.

Princess Mariposa turned to him. A blank expression filled her face. Her usually sapphire eyes turned a dark sea green.

Prince Baltazar shuffled his boots. "If I may be excused," he began.

"You are excused," Princess Mariposa said in a toneless voice.

Prince Baltazar bowed and then left in a hurry.

I remained glued to my spot. I wasn't leaving unless the Princess herself ordered me to. I gazed up at Prince Humphrey—the Humphrey who'd given the Princess the beautiful butterfly, the Humphrey who'd been a spoiled brat—with my mouth hanging open.

He winked at me.

"Tubby?" Princess Mariposa repeated as if she couldn't wrap her mind around the thought. "It's been you all along?"

Prince Humphrey winced. "Don't remind me of how rotten I behaved back then."

"Yes, you were rotten," she agreed, a little pink color returning to her face.

"I wanted you to like me and I didn't know how to get you to. I sent you a butterfly."

She nodded. "I still have it."

"You do?" he asked, smiling. "I'm sorry, Mariposa, sorry for pretending to be someone else, but I wanted to see you again. And I wasn't sure I'd be welcome." He reached out and took her hands. "Forgive me?"

"Forgive you?" she mused. "For what? Pulling my hair? Pretending to be a poor nobody? Ruining my wedding? Preventing me from marrying an imposter?"

"For not visiting you sooner," Prince Humphrey said.

At that, a smile curled the corner of the Princess's mouth.

"I suppose," she said. "I forgive you. Just this once."

Prince Humphrey laughed. "And now that we're

friends," he said as Princess Mariposa arched an eyebrow, "perhaps you'd introduce me to your servant here."

Princess Mariposa looked down at me, blinking as if she'd forgotten I was there.

"This is my friend Darling," she said.

My heart swelled; I was Princess Mariposa's friend.

"Pleased to make your acquaintance," Prince Humphrey said with a bow.

I curtsied. "The pleasure is all mine."

"Darling," Princess Mariposa said. "Don't miss out on lunch."

I curtsied again and walked off, glancing back every few steps.

A large blue butterfly fluttered down between them. Princess Mariposa studied it. It hovered a moment before sailing off.

"I saw an *Inachis io* once," she said, watching it go.

"Did you catch it?" Prince Humphrey asked, offering her his arm.

"No," Princess Mariposa said. "I let it go."

Then she took his arm and the two strolled back toward the castle, a rainbow of butterflies following in their wake.

35

The Guards scoured the castle from the attics to the cellars. There was no sign of Cherice. In all the excitement, she had escaped. The wedding festivities continued despite the fact that there hadn't been a wedding. The food was superb; the fireworks extravagant. The servants, awarded a break from their duties, watched from the lawns. The party went on for days.

At last, the guests departed; Prince Baltazar was the first to go. He invited Princess Mariposa to visit Candala at her convenience.

"Like that will happen," Lindy said, pressing a nightgown. "Candala might be paradise, but Her Highness would rather die than set foot in it after what that scoundrel Dudley did to humiliate her."

"Do you think the gryphon ate him?" I asked, wincing.

"Darlin'," Lindy said, "don't go imagining things you oughtn't to imagine. The masons will patch up that turret and we'll *all* forget it ever happened."

I didn't argue with her, but I doubted it. The two of us staggered under the heavy load of pressing the Princess's wardrobe, which was left unattended now that Cherice was gone. Iago poked his nose in the pressing room from time to time, but he always shook his head at the ever-growing pile of dresses, stockings, and petticoats that needed sorting and putting away. Then he vanished back into his haven under my bed.

Finally, the Baroness Azure offered her assistance. She was, I learned, the first peer of the realm, the richest lady at court. Armed with her cane, she planted herself in an armchair and rattled off orders like a general. Lindy and I—along with Francesca, whom the Baroness had recruited to help—scurried to obey. Princess Mariposa couldn't find a new Wardrobe Mistress soon enough, in my opinion.

Mrs. Pepperwhistle looked in on us occasionally. Her gaze reflected the hunger she felt for her daughter's advancement. No doubt she thought Francesca should step right into Cherice's shoes, but the Baroness spent her time in between issuing orders compiling a list of candidates that she believed were suitable for the position.

It was a long list. I didn't see Francesca's name any-where on it.

"Marci, the Head Scrubber, would be good at this job," I told the Baroness one afternoon when she ordered me to rub her feet. I wrinkled my nose against the smell of her stockings and rubbed away.

"Marci?" the Baroness snorted.

"Her grandmother was Queen Paloma's Wardrobe Mistress. I guess she taught Marci everything she knew," I replied.

"Marci has a temper," Lindy said, walking past.

"So do you," I mumbled under my breath.

The Baroness cackled, eyes bright with glee. "Does she?"

"They both do," I whispered. "Good servants are jeal-ous of their work."

"Are you?" she asked, eyes twinkling.

"Yes," I said with a nod.

"Then rub harder," the Baroness murmured, closing her eyes.

It was days later that I realized something. Something important. When a strange mouse popped up and wrote Roger a note telling him I was in danger, he hadn't hesi-tated to come to my rescue. Maybe he did like me—a little anyway. At least we were still friends.

Gillian sidled up to me one evening on the east terrace.

"You haven't told me a story in weeks," she whined.

"I haven't seen any soap bubbles lately," I said, leaning back into the bronze lion's chest.

The days had grown cooler; it would probably be the last evening out on the lawn until next spring.

"Come on," Gillian moaned.

"Well," I said, studying my fingernails. "There once was a girl who had to scrub the floors in a witch's castle. Every day, she scrubbed, dragging a heavy bucket, a rag in her reddened fist, all alone."

"Oh," Gillian breathed, settling in with her chin on her fist. "Yes, go on."

Jane sat down next to me and squeezed my knee.

"Good evening," she said.

"Hi, Jane. What will you and the other Pickers do when it's colder?" I asked.

Gillian squirmed like a fly caught in a spider's web.

"We can always help out in the greenhouses. They grow lots of things in there—flowers, vegetables, fruit trees," she answered.

"Really?" I said as if I wanted to hear more.

"What about the girl in the witch's castle?" Gillian said, poking me.

"She was caught slacking and sent to bed without her supper," Marci said, plopping down on the other side of Jane.

Gillian shriveled up like a wilted lettuce leaf.

A falling star streaked through the night sky.

"Make a wish," Marci told Jane.

Jane smiled, her cheeks pink, her eyes hazy. "What would I wish for? I have my girl," she said, squeezing me.

"I'd wish for a story," Gillian grumbled under her breath.

"I'd wish that the hidden things would become known," Marci said, glancing at Jane and nudging her apron pocket. "It's about time they were."

Jane frowned, squinting at the stars and patting her pocket.

"Come on, Janey," Marci said. "Let her have it. She's earned it. She ran out in front of that monster to warn the Princess. She's entitled to a reward."

"Let me have what?" I asked.

Jane sighed. She dug in her pocket and brought out her closed fist.

"I meant for you to have this," Jane said.

"Just give it to her," Marci urged.

Gillian leaned over my shoulder, eager to see what Jane had in her fist.

"I'm giving it to her. Do you mind?" Jane said.

"Just tell me what it is," I suggested.

"It belonged to your mother," Jane said, her voice failing.

"Oh," I said.

I never thought about my mother. She'd died the day I was born; she'd never been there when I needed her.

"It belonged to her family, passed down for generations. She left it with me, to give to you," Jane said, shoulders drooping. She thrust her hand out at me. "Take it. It's yours."

A thin silver chain glinted in Jane's hand. A silver locket dangled from it. I put out my hand and she let it fall into my grasp. I studied it. The locket had a starburst engraved on one side and on the other the word WRAY.

"Wray?" Gillian asked. "What's that?" She dug her chin into my shoulder, straining for a better look.

I nudged her off me.

"It's your mother's family name. She was a Wray, Emily Wray," Jane admitted as if it killed her to do so.

"So your name's really Darling Wray," Gillian said. "That sounds more romantic than Darling Dimple."

"Her father's name wasn't Wray," Marci objected.

"What was it?" Gillian demanded.

"James Fortune," Jane said.

"Darling Fortune? That's almost as good as Darling Dimple!" Gillian snorted.

"Captain James Fortune," Marci amended.

I opened the locket. It was empty.

"I'm sorry, Darling," Jane murmured. "I should have told you. I should have given you the locket long ago."

Marci harrumphed.

"Why didn't you?" I asked.

Jane twisted her fingers together. "Well," she said, "I was an orphan. My aunt Doris raised me. She was the Head Icer—she made the most beautiful sugar roses. I grew up here in the castle. But I never had anything. My aunt died years ago and, well, I didn't have a family of my own—"

"So you took care of me," I said. "But you never told me you were an orphan."

"I'm not an orphan," Gillian announced.

"No," said Marci, "just a girl who talks too much."

"So I pretended that you were really my little girl," Jane finished with a sob.

The castle lawn spun around me. I wasn't Darling Dimple, not really. I was somebody whose mother had been a Wray. Somebody who'd inherited a silver locket with a starburst—the same starburst the west terrace bore. Suddenly, I felt all alone. A stranger. A nobody.

Jane squeezed me as silent tears ran down her face. Good old Jane. Jane, who'd taught me to read and write. Jane, who'd loved me every day of my life. I didn't know Emily Wray or Captain James Fortune, but I knew Jane.

"I am your girl," I told her.

She kissed the top of my head. I tightened my fist around the locket. Overhead the stars twinkled in the night sky. Marci poked an errant strand of hair back into her bun. Other servants, eager to enjoy a last evening on the lawn, came out with their shawls and scarves. Their soft chatter filled the night air.

I polished the locket on my apron; finally I had a treasure of my own to put in my artichoke crate. But for now, I intended to wear it. I slipped the chain over my head and settled into Jane's side. I didn't know who Emily Wray was or what her starburst locket meant or if it had ever held anything, but I intended to find out. Someday. For now, I was Darling Dimple, Jane's girl, and I had a great story to tell.

"So," I told Gillian, "one day an unusually large soap bubble floated out of the girl's bucket. It got stuck in a shaft of sunlight."

"Yeah?" Gillian breathed in the dark.

"And inside the bubble was a genie."

"A genie? Oh. What's next?" Gillian said with a sigh.

So I told her the story about the genie and the thousand magic slippers and how the little Scrubber girl danced in a different pair each night until she wore a hole in the floor and fell through. And then her adventure really began.

Acknowledgments

Books are written, but they are also made. I would like to thank the many people whose work, kindness, and inspiration went into the making of this book. My agent, Sara Crowe, who never stopped believing I could do this. My editor, Diane Landolf, for believing in Darling and her dresses. My book designer, Liz Tardiff, and all the other people at Random House who have labored over this book and made it the beautiful object you hold in your hands.

To my critique partners, Kaye Bair and Rachel Martin, for patiently reading and rereading, and offering helpful insights and suggestions, and asking difficult-to-answer questions. To the "Ames" group—Sarvinder Naberhaus, Jane Metcalf, Candace Camling, Dorothia Rohner, Lisa Victoria, Kate Sharp, Ann Green—for all their support.

To my husband, Jon, and my daughters, Sara and Becky, for indulging my obsession.

And to all the authors of my favorite books—you taught me how to imagine all the things that weren't. And to God, who whispered to me that the things that weren't could *be*.